To Arthur,

New

EDEN'S OUTCAST

KUTA MARLER

EDEN'S OUTCAST
Copyright © 2018 Kuta Marler

ISBN: 978-0-692-13636-2

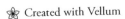 Created with Vellum

1

FRY SAUCE

He held her memories in his hands. Lilith watched him as he flipped through the pages of the dragon skin bound journal, the skin's magic preserved her memories and protected them. She did not enjoy dying, and coming back to life always hurt. But not even death could take away the time she had spent roaming the world as long as she wrote it down. With a stroke of her pen she decided what remained in her narrative. She couldn't decide what to do about Zech, the gentleman who sat across the table from her. He was so stinking cute, and yet he would be so difficult to kill.

The diner was decked out with Americana, porcelain signage advertising refreshing beverages. Another held the forced smile of a housewife embossed on tin. Century old ads still, Lilith was older than everything on the walls. Wide windows showed the traffic passing by on State St. Down the road sat the Lehi Roller Mill. Lilith could remember when fields stretched for miles around the mill. Now stores and restaurants seemed to be stacked on top of each other. Snowcapped mountains silhouetted by the sun were also younger than the woman with gray skin who sat in the red vinyl booth. The waitress and the cook were nowhere to be seen.

Lilith had wasted hours trying to figure out why the stupid

angel hadn't tried to kill her. The vinyl squeaked beneath her as she shifted her hips. She eyed the remains of the fry sauce, a strange mix of mayo and ketchup, she hated the taste but loved the texture across her tongue.

Despite all this, Lilith and Zech looked like a normal couple, even comfortable.

"Go on then," Zech said.

He smiled as Lilith picked up the fry sauce container devouring the plastic cup. He sounded like he was mumbling as he spoke, "You could devour the world."

"And still be hungry." Lilith's rich voice dripped like the fry sauce that had flowed down her throat. She smacked her lips, eying the ketchup bottle.

"Come on. You don't want to attract any undue attention. Let's head over to your place." Zech waggled dark black brows at her.

"Me and you?" Lilith scoffed. She wouldn't admit to actually entertaining the idea.

"It's happened before." Zech leaned forward with a half-smile and locked eyes with her.

Lilith looked away. "Funny, I'd remember sleeping with the enemy."

"I'm not the one with a ticklish bum." He smiled.

She crinkled her nose. *How'd he know?*

"I also know which scars are new and which ones are original. All of them." He winked at her.

"What'd you want Zech? Besides the obvious," Lilith asked. She leaned back crossing her arms over her chest.

"Cain's skull."

Lilith blinked twice and pursed her lips. "You want the skull of my dead brother?"

"Are you using it?" Zech asked closing the journal and putting it down on the dirty table.

"No." Lilith shook her head.

"Let me borrow it then. I promise to return it."

"I'm not in the habit of keeping the skulls of my loved ones."

Lilith reached out and pulled her journal across the table, sliding it inside the pocket in her maroon coat.

"We all handle grief in our own way Lilith." Zech reached out across the table resting a tan hand on her gray skin. Electricity prickled across Lilith's skin as he spoke. "Also you may have mentioned a box at another time."

"Why would I leave you out of my journal?" she asked. She pulled her hand away. Lilith put everyone in her journals, and he knew too much about her. Yet nothing came to mind. She could smell traces of angel on the cover of her journal, angels smelt of sweet chili pepper. *He probably tastes amazing. but maybe a little stringy.*

"Unable to find the right words to describe our chemistry I suppose. We've left a trail of natural disasters throughout history. There are a couple that I'm personally fond of, like the time in New Zealand." The setting sun backlit him in the booth giving him a halo of light on a tumble of curly black hair. Amber eyes seemed to dissect and weigh her.

Zech irked her. A scrawny irksome angel would not have escaped the page. She'd stuck around because this was the first angel that hadn't attempted to kill her on sight and he had offered to buy dinner. "Or you're not worth the ink."

Thunder rolled across the mountain front. "They're playing my song." Zech stood and dropped a couple of bills on the table.

Lilith shuddered. Thunder meant another angel was nearby.

"I've missed you Lil." He leaned in close brushing a loose strand of ashen hair away from her face. Her skin tingled where his fingers crossed her skin. A bright flash of light filled her sight. An empty diner appeared as she regained her vision. Zech had left the building. Lilith hands searched her jacket for a pen—her journal heavy in her pocket—when a low growl interrupted her.

On the table in front of her sat a hodag scratching at the back of his head with a hind leg. Black obsidian claws clinking against emerald green scales. No bigger than a lap dog. The creature on the table had a perpetual grin due to a multitude of bright white fangs filling its mouth. Opalescent spittle dribbled down its lip. Zech had dropped a hodag in front of her when he left. "Stupid Kiwi." The first flightless bird that came to mind slipped out of her mouth. Angels couldn't fly even though they desperately wanted their wings.

Lilith glanced over to the kitchen, the remainder of the diner was clear. She asked the creature in front of her, "What are you doing west of the Mississippi?"

The hodag lunged for her, acidic drool sizzled the paper mat. The drool melted her sternum, waves of pain spread from her chest. She scowled down at the little monster whose head had disappeared into her cleavage.

Sharp teeth began to prick at her heart. *Never trust an angel.*

Her hand wrapped around the butter knife and she plunged it into the base of the monster's neck as she died. She slid forward, it looked as if she was cuddling a cherished pet as she perished.

Lilith gasped and pulled air into fresh lungs.

She'd been talking to someone. She opened her journal, no notes on who it could've been.

In front of her a decapitated hodag slumped on her dinner plate.

She gave a deep sniff, some of her blood drifted through now still veins. "You must be why I died. Guess I'll be taking you to go." She grabbed the hodag like a child holding a teddy bear. The creatures blood had burned through her shirt and decimated her bra. Her dark red jacket had been left unscathed. She pulled the useless bra off leaving it on the table. "That'll be one hell of a tip to explain." She grinned, wondering where the staff had gone.

She grabbed the little monster by the tail and tipped it up drinking deeply from its neck. Fire burned down her throat. The feeling could've been mistaken for excruciating heartburn. "Not my favorite meal." Lilith said. She took a big bite out of the raw jade flesh.

She walked out of the diner into an empty parking lot and a chorus of howls broke out behind her.

Packs, hodags traveled in packs. She booked it down the road.

"Come on, Lilith," she muttered to herself. "Do you really want to die again tonight?" She needed to get back to her house, if she could find it. She read a license plate. Utah. "Ugh." She rolled her eyes. "At least I'm in the right state."

The snow dusted mountains behind her reached up and touched the inky sky. Lilith could remember when this was all underwater and giant scaled monstrosities swam beneath the surface of the sea. She ran on the shoulder of the road, gravel crunching under heavy leather boots. She couldn't remember what she was doing in the state, probably something to do with whoever she was talking to in the diner.

The area near her house (at least where she *thought* her house was) was now covered in homes. They invaded the landscape sprawling like a fungus. It had been a few years —ok a little more than a few since she had been back. Between the memory loss that happened when she died and the ever-changing landscape, Lilith was lost.

Members of the pack started appearing out of the shadows. She threw the remainder of the hodag in her hand behind her. The pack stopped for a moment to devour what she hadn't been able to stomach. Teeth, claws and bones. The snarls and growls of the hodags made her consider breaking into one of the darkened houses to shake the creatures off her trail.

She ached from the first death of the night which she blamed on the pack, at least one of them. Damn thing had eaten her heart. She had no desire to pass through the digestive tract of the little monsters.

That would require a lot of hunting and hodags tasted of bile and sulfur. Not good eats. She had eaten one, that was more than enough.

She considered leading the lot of them through the new houses, but they might not have owners yet. If they were empty that would leave her with no one to disembowel as distraction for the pack. Hodags tracked by smell. The new heart ached with every beat, like searing needles of pain. The joy of regeneration, this one would ache for months, another death would add to the latent pain.

She giggled as the memory of the lumberjack lying to the

Smithsonian about Hodags filtered back in. Also it was rare to see them out of Wisconsin. She wasn't sure how they had got hold of her scent but she'd find a way to shake them.

The wind shifted her tattered shirt. A car coming towards her swerved and honked. *I guess more of my shirt is missing then I realized.* She may not be able to do anything about the lack of support but she could find a shirt, probably. She took a left and hopped a white metal gate, above her letters spelled out "North County Equestrian Park." As she approached the large gray shed, she checked behind her, two--no three—emerald darts moved.

The smell of partially digested grass mixed with gastric juices hit Lilith.

Manure.

"That might work. Eh, worth a try." The process of death didn't bother Lilith, on occasion she enjoyed dying. That one blissful moment of nothing she wished to exist in before she lived again.

Lilith threw her shoulder against a side door and tumbled into a room full of tack and gear. She dropped her jacket and ripped the tattered remains of her shirt off. Even a horse blanket would be better than that rag. A starched white collared dress shirt hung on the back wall. Lilith pulled the shirt down off the wall. She tugged off her jacket. "Fancy." She pulled on the shirt ran tight in the shoulders but it would do.

She pulled a bucket of feed over spilling the oats on the ground. "Snack time." Though the hodags preferred her flesh. "And some for me." She munched on a handful of oats Not the best, but food is food. She slipped her jacket back on, checking for her journal, she then passed through another door into the arena.

Blue light cut in through the clear corrugated plexiglass, casting geometric shapes over the sawdust-filled oval pen. Metal stadium lined the arena.

Lilith tripped, falling into the sawdust, a billow of it swirling up around her. Instead of pulling herself up she rolled around on the ground, grabbed a dark lump of hard horse manure with a gloved hand, and rubbed it over her clothes like soap. Taking extra care to scrub it on the gray skin of her neck before mashing the rest through her ashen hair. The white pressed shirt now stained with dark streaks of horse manure.

She paused a moment, expecting to hear snacking in the next room. The wind creaked through a large sliding door at the end of the giant training shed. The blue light shifted over the floor. The wall squeaked and she grabbed for her knife from the sheath she kept on the back of her belt. The strange warped pattern etched in the blade caught the blue light. Nothing but the wind moved in the wide arena. *They probably found a snack, might as well take a break while I wait. No use running just now.*

Lilith yawned, put away the knife, and went up the bleachers. If the hodags were going to keep her waiting, she could at least catch her breath. She pulled out her journal flipping it open and thumbing the pages, *only a few left in this one.* She needed to make a new journal, soon. She scribbled a quick note. *Hodags: in Utah. Don't forget the packs.* She put the book away, stretching her arms till her shoulder popped. *Now if I could remember where my house is.*

The house would turn up –it always did. It never moved but, the world around it changed and warped, leaving it like her, a stranger in a more complex world.

She stood up and walked along the top bench. As she pivoted on her foot and twirled she tripped a little, arms flailing as she caught her balance. She looked down to the ground. *That would be a nasty spill.* She took a step down, considered for a moment falling, and the quiet that followed.

A rattle hauled her back to the present moment.

As she turned towards the noise, the back of her knees hit the bench, and she toppled over the bleachers, one foot catching, leaving her dangling twenty feet above the ground. Her jacket wrapped around her face, strangling her, and restricting her breath. She clawed at it trying to remove it from her head.

In the struggle, her foot came loose and she plummeted to the ground. *This is going to suck.* Her skull hit the ground. She could feel the vertebrae in her upper neck crush and grind against the others, a sharp pain cutting through her neck. Her body crumpled flat on the ground. *Not again. I hate breaking my neck.*

Worse than the pain was the spreading numbness that ate away her ability to move. Her heartbeat sounding in her ears slowed, and then stopped. The peace tried to consume her, but the time with it felt shorter than before.

Another day, another death.

A dark green, scaled shadow wiggled through the corrugated-metal wall of the arena. It sniffed and huffed through the sawdust tracing the now-deceased Lilith's trail, scuttling up until it reached the top of the bleachers. The small scaled dog-like creature howled, calling to the rest of the pack.

Lilith gasped as air filled her lungs. At least she'd been able to skip the pain of her vertebrae knitting back together, however pain still radiated from her neck. This one more intense than the pang from her heart.

Yep, regeneration still sucks.

Her joints throbbed, and her bones crackled as if on fire. Agony and hunger were the only real consequence for Lilith when she died.

I was running from something... Her memories hadn't quite come back yet, coming back from the dead was like waking up with a hangover.

Agony and fog.

She looked up toward the metal bleachers and a toothy, fanged smile grinned down from above, large deep-set yellow eyes watching for movement.

"Right. Hodags." The problem with regeneration was that it smelled horrid —of rotten eggs —and added bonus, it attracted unnatural creatures.

A second hodag arrived, this one sniffing around the ground nearby.

Lilith jumped up.

It came up to her shin. Obsidian claws pawed at the ground and, as it looked up at her with that ridiculous grin, teeth gnashed and ground together.

Meat, she thought. *I need to find them meat!*

2
ENTER THE DAME

John smiled. Recalling how Sarah kissed him goodbye before she'd left for the night.

So much studying to do, he reminded himself, *no time for day dreaming.* A frown settled on his round face.

If Mike bothered to show up for his shift, John would already be home. Stupid desks at the Plasma Center, standing up to use them hurt his feet. Sitting wasn't an option.

Six donors remained. In less than five minutes, he could lock the doors for the night.

John distracted himself by shuffling some files across the top of the desk, like playing cards in a magic trick.

Mark came out from the donor bays behind John, sneakers squeaking across the linoleum, pulling at the lab coat that constantly slipped off his weak shoulders. "Georgie!"

"Please, don't call me that," John said. He hated his first name, George, for St. George the dragon slayer. As a kid he knew everything about dragons and supernatural creatures, from the myths to the real-life inspirations.

He'd grown out of that phase when he realized he'd be better off saving people in the medical field instead of slaying komodo dragons. John, while a generic middle name, he didn't mind so much.

"It's the final countdown. Do you want me to handle closing tonight?" Mark asked.

"No. Thanks for the offer." John said, the files seemed to beg to be put away. Instead he scratched at a scaly patch of skin on his elbow.

Mark leaned on the counter. "Any word on that shift switch?"

"Yep. I've got you covered," John said, stacking the files.

Mark fist-pumped the air, shaggy black hair falling in his face. "You are a saint! Thank you!"

"Do you have any idea what happened to Mike tonight?" John asked running a hand through short brown hair. "He was supposed to close, dontcha know?"

"Your Minnesotan is showing," Mark said, coming around the desk.

John stepped out of the way of the tubby guy.

Mark grabbed the files and put them away. "Not sure what happened. If you don't mind, I'll start working on boxing the plasma for today."

"Sounds like a plan." John didn't want to handle the bottles of yellow plasma for shipping. He might be able to sneak his text book out and get a few pages of reading done at the desk.

"Thanks." Mark gave him a nod before disappearing into the back.

A strange prickling ran across the back of John's neck. He rubbed at the skin, trying to chase it away. "Well, it could be worse," he said pulling out an allen-key from the drawer and walking towards the front door.

Outside the glass, a gray shadow charged towards him. *What the hell is that?* he wondered, clenching the key in his hand.

A woman in utter disarray, stormed through the double doors. John blinked, because at first, she appeared cloudy under the fluorescent lights, translucent even. Loose ashen hair flowed behind her. Dressed in dirty, dark denim jeans, a dress shirt that might have been white once, and a red coat, the arm tattered and torn, she looked a mess. Half of her left boot was missing.

The smell of horse crap and dirt flooded in with her. She

charged towards him in the confined space between the two sets of glass doors. John scuttled out of the way and took refuge behind his desk. *Give her some armor and a sword and she could be a Shield maiden.*

"Barricade that door!" she commanded. Her good boot stomped across the gray-flecked white tile. While the tongue of her bad boot flopped out like a dog panting. John would have ignored her, but the odd hunting knife in her hand labeled her as a threat. The blade itself dripped with a strange jade goo that sizzled as it hit the floor.

John took a breath and tried to remember what the management training videos had said about armed assailants. *Probably should have stayed awake for those.* "Why?" he asked, looking behind her out into the empty parking lot. Something skittered under a car, probably a rat, nothing to be alarmed about. Right?

His stomach churned, chest tightening. He recoiled as she waved the knife around the contained space. He ran back to his desk, picked up the phone, and began to dial 9, 1–.

The woman flicked her knife sending a glob of jade goo flying, which landed on the number pad. It sparked, sizzled, and then melted in front of him. The dial tone died. He held the receiver in his hand, the cable swung in front of him like a pendulum.

"Cops are a bad idea." She returned her attention to the front door.

He dropped the receiver. John felt like the woman in front of him had just scuttled his lifeboat. He reached for his cellphone, but the battery had died.

Stay calm. His neck twitched as he edged away from her.

The woman turned on her heel facing him, knife in hand.

Of all the nights to be shift manager, John stood behind the desk. Had anyone else noticed her?

A gangly donor walked into the front lobby, his glazed look common just after donation. *Apparently not.* The donor rubbed at a hawkish nose and moved towards the front door, taking his time as he left the building. Dark hair trimmed short, his steel blue eyes registered the knife.

He stopped, then lunged for the door. The woman tried to intercept him, but missed.

"Come back here," she said.

The donor pulled open the inner set of doors of the building escaping into the outer lobby. A tug of war began between the woman and the donor over the door. Each time he succeeded in closing the inside set of doors, the air puffed, opening the outside one which now hung a few inches ajar. The donor had trapped himself. If he let go, she'd get him, but he couldn't get away either.

A scaled, green creature on all fours zipped through the outer door. It sniffed at the donor's calf. Then tipping up it's muzzle it howled.

A high pitched painful noise that forced John to cover his ears. The creature's fanged smile grew wide. A matching shriek came out of the donor when he turned and faced the little monster.

The first monster to enter cocked his head in response and howled again.

A second cry brought ten others bursting through the outer doors, a landslide of obsidian claws and fangs. The first creature jumped, scrambling up the donor's chest and perched on his shoulder.

It glared at John through the glass. John stumbled back, colliding with something. The file cabinet squealed behind him as it shifted on the floor. Heart racing, blood pumping he bite his tongue keeping himself from screaming.

One creature bit the donor's pant leg. The jean turned from blue to maroon. In a rush, the other creatures pounced on him – like ants amassing on a fallen potato chip.

The donor disappeared in a sea of writhing green. Crimson splatters flicked across the glass, making an unholy mosaic of flesh and blood. In a matter of seconds he was gone—consumed by the little monstrosities—and leaving nothing but glittering eyes and blood stained teeth on the other side of the glass. John gasped trying to comprehend what happened.

The woman stopped trying to open the door. John hoped the woman had been trying to save the donor. The frame of the doors shivered with every hit from the pack; onyx claws scraped against the glass, clearing streaks in the mess they had made, spit and blood flicking from their mouths. They were still hungry.

John slid down to the ground and hid beneath the tall desk. The blood shuddered in the veins of his neck.

"Oi, Meat, hiding beneath the table. Mind coming out and giving me a hand?" The tall woman asked from the door.

John peeked over the desktop. "Are you going to hurt me?"

"I'm trying to save you." The door shuddered against her hold as the green monsters hit the glass, repeatedly. "Stupid Hodags."

"Oh," John said, there must have been something intelligent to say, but John's mind couldn't make heads or tails of what just happened.

"If you like living come help me."

"Right," John stood up on shaky legs and headed over to the door.

"Can you manage to lock the door?" She asked.

"Uh, yeah," John said. He opened a trembling hand revealing the allen key.

He stumbled towards her, shying away from the knife in her hand and released the bar lock on the door. The creatures on the other side snarled and growled at him as he flicked the black switch at the top of the door to keep the handicap button from operating. Vibrant green four legged creatures coated with splattered patterns of scarlet flopped and rolled around on the floor mat playing like pupppies. "You said 'Hodags' Like the Wisconsin hoax?"

"Hoax?" Lilith asked. "I always wondered what that old lumberjack had said about them."

John's family had driven through Rhinelander Wisconsin once, home of the mischievous hodag. The hodag had been stitched together of random parts by a local lumberjack and turned out to be a prank. "A lot smaller than the statue." John stepped back as a tongue lapped blood off the glass. He shuddered.

"Come on," The woman grabbed him by the arm. "Help me move that filing cabinet over." Together they grabbed the cabinet and hauled it over to the door.

"Explain," he said. pointing at the shaking door. "Please?"

"Not a hoax. Real," she said. "And meat. They love meat."

John's stomach clenched. "Meat?" he asked. "Does that include people?"

"Are people made of meat?" she said gesturing at the bloody mosaic that was sliding off the door and onto the floor. "They love to eat people. If you couldn't tell."

"We need to get them away from the plasma center," John said. He used his backside to scoot the cabinet closer to the door. "You're here to help me, right?"

The woman dropped her blade to her side. She leaned in closer and cocked her head, staring at him, brow furrowing. "Have you always had blue eyes?"

John leaned back, the cabinet pressing into his back, "Uh, yes." The smell of iron and dirt drifting towards him, and... was that manure? *Wait, is she flirting with me? In the middle of a disaster?*

"You smell odd, she said. As if checking off another item on a list of requirements.

John frowned, and gave his shirt a sniff. Nothing unusual.

She turned away as if conversing with herself until, shrugging her shoulders, she turned back. "Yeah, why not?" A thud from the front foyer interrupted her. "Tell me, what other exits are there?"

"Exit at the back of the donor bays," he said looking towards the back where the donors were. "Then the front door and an emergency exit in the break room."

"We'll need bait to get out of here." The woman stared at John.

John felt as if he'd been sized and weighed. "Will plasma work?"

"If you have a large amount and help me carry it." She smiled. "As long as the rest of the meat stays back there they'll be fine."

"They're called people," John said. *The way she talks you'd think she wasn't human.*

"As far as the hodags are concerned, they're called meat." She peeked over his shoulder. The front lobby silent, the door still. "Where on earth did they go?" she asked.

"That's not a good thing," John eyed the knife. "Will you put the knife away? You'll be less imposing without it."

"Fine," she said pouting like a child. Wiping the knife on the counter, the remaining goo sizzled and ate away at the surface. She stuck the knife in a sheath at the back of her belt.

"Nice to see you can be reasoned with. Come on." John pressed forward, he could feel the blood racing through his neck. *Don't freak out now. Freak out later,* he chanted in his head. He ran past a privacy screen, and saw Iris. A gray bun crowned her head: she was kneeling restocking a cart, her lab coat draped across the floor like a royal robe.

"Iris!" John came up behind her and put his hand on her shoulder.

She jumped. "Oh! John. You startled me." She put a hand to her chest and pulled herself up using the counter. "You're so quiet." Iris fell to one side, a hand out toward the strange woman, then stumbled back into the supply cart.

The gray woman held up a hand, "Easy."

Iris nodded, biting her lower lip, wrinkles pulled across her chin. Iris looked the woman in the eye and spoke, in a flat tone, "Hag."

John's brow creased and jaw dropped. "Iris!"

The hag waved her hand dismissing the slight. "Now that we all know each other. Iris why don't you fetch me a couple of bottles of plasma."

Iris took off to the boxing room.

3
SOMETHING WICKED

Hag?" John asked.

"Eh, it works." she shrugged.

"I'm not calling you that." Above John on the other side of the ceiling panels, something thumped along a support beam. His eyes widened. He felt his gut drop. "Is that them?"

The Hag sighed, tapping her blade on the wall. "Probably."

I'm so glad Sarah isn't here. John heard clawing coming from the other side of the wall, and jumped away. Small ruptures appeared in the sheet rock. He looked up when bits of plaster flaked off the molding, drifting down toward him like macabre snow.

A ceiling panel fell to the floor revealing a dozen glowing yellow eyes, all lined up in the darkness above. A shower of green came tumbling out, spilling across the floor. The hodags fanned out, sniffing the ground and licking anything that contained traces of blood.

At the sight of the invading mass, the remaining employees started taking lines out of donors. One donor in fright, yanked his out, the blood spraying from his arm.

John ran over to him. "Apply pressure." He grabbed a handful of gauze pressing it to the sight where the needle had been. The little beasts snapped and growled, darting around the room as if trying to herd a flock of frightened geese.

A hodag pulled at the abandoned intake tube still attached to a machine. It shook the line splattering blood across the floor. Bright crimson smeared beneath his hind paws.

John cringed. His heart beat thudded in his ears, while he managed quick shallow breaths. The machine began to tilt and fell on top of the hodag with a crunch.

Its eyes bulged as it squirmed and struggled to get out from under. Pulling itself out, it limped along to join the rest of the pack. Two other hodags flanked it, pounced, and devoured their injured companion.

Another monster used the fallen machine to leap onto a supply cart. The little-nasty batted a bright neon-pink wrap around the top of the cart, like a cat with a ball of yarn. He bit into the wrap, sticky pink threads wrapping around its teeth and gumming up its jaw, like a pack of bubblegum.

The Hag jabbed John with the butt of her blade. "Do you want to be on the menu?"

John gulped. "No."

"Do you like animals?" The Hag asked.

"Yes, just not the ones that will eat me," John said.

Iris came back her arms filled with plasma bottles.

The Hag grabbed the bottles. Using one hand she popped the lid off. "Think of it this way. These are animals you've never seen before. I'll teach you how to handle them. Iris get everyone else out of the way."

Iris nodded and began to shepherd donors and employees towards the break room.

John threw his hands up in the air, "Next you'll tell me the whole murderous pack can be put up for adoption."

The woman glared at John. Looked him square in the eyes and dumped the open bottle of plasma on his head. She grabbed another bottle and did the same to herself. Then took her blade and ran it down the length of her forearm, shredding through what remained of the coat, blue blood oozed from the cut.

His stomach roiled as she bled the wrong color. The skin stitched back together right before his eyes. The blue blood and plasma swirled together on the knife's edge and she wiped it across John's chest.

She said, "I'll need that back."

"What?" John jumped away from the woman. He caught a whiff of the dark blue blood. It smelled, wrong, like rotten apples mixed with raw beef.

"The blood. I'll need my blood back." She licked what remained off the edge of the blade.

John shuddered, wiping plasma out of his eyes.

"Run." Yellow plasma dripped off her nose. She took off and headed for the front door. "You are being lousy bait."

The skittering of claws behind him prompted his legs to work. He passed through one set of doors and then out into the crisp night air.

"Do you think this will work?" John asked. He could feel his calves beginning to burn.

"Don't know. I thought the smell of the donors would throw them, but looks like it just made them hungry." She started to laugh. "Oops."

"You brought them here?" John asked. The ache had moved up his legs. "On purpose? Are you insane?"

"Yes, yes, and yes." The hag lead them into an orchard behind the Plasma Center. Fermented fruit permeated the air. John's shoes squelched in the soft earth. The hag scooped up a rotted apple and took a bite.

"Gross!"

"Got to snack when I can." She finished up the apple, core crunching beneath her teeth.

A snarl reminded John that they were being hunted.

John lost his balance and barreled into The Hag and they tumbled down a slope together. The slope cut off into a sharp ridge, leaving them to fall three feet. He hit the ground with a thud landing on top of the woman. A loud crack came from her ribcage a split formed on her forehead and a trickle of blood moved slowly down and across her brow.

"I don't want to die again," she said, her eyes unfocusing.

"Again?" John asked. He turned and looked up at the top of the hill, a dozen yellow eyes appeared, bobbing in the night. It was hard to get a count of how many little monsters were up there. "Oh, crap."

He watched as the hodags scale down the ridge wall, like the ridge had pulsing green veins. The leaves rustled as the monsters closed in on their location. The woman groaned trying to get up off the ground and fell back down into the damp soil.

John grabbed a large branch and bracing himself for the upcoming fight.

Two hodags flanked him.

He swung the branch down hitting one creature square in the forehead. Its tongue rolled out of its mouth.

The Hag forced herself up. She pulled out her blade. "You should've kept running." The woman plunged her blade into the neck of the second hodag.

"And let you die?"

"Yes."

His forehead furrowed at her response. "You know the appropriate response would be, 'Hey, John, thanks for rescuing me.'"

The rest of the creatures darted through the apple trees above. "Come on, let's get you out of here." He hoisted her up and threw her arm over his shoulder starting back to the center. He may not be faster than the hodags but his car would be.

John felt as if he was hauling bags of cement. "Woah, you are heavy."

"Do you have a death wish?" Lilith snarled.

She stumbled forward. The hodags vanished into the orchard trees behind the plasma center.

John figured anything that hungry couldn't be far away.

"Going back to the center is a bad idea. You don't want hodags setting up a nest." She pitched forward out of his arms. A black journal slid out of her jacket and hit the ground. "Stop!"

"We need to keep moving," John said trying to pull her along.

"Not without my journal," her words were short as if she'd lost her breath.

"A journal isn't worth dying over," John said.

She struggled out of his grasp and slipped from his arms onto the ground. Her knife fell from her hands. John grabbed the blade, feeling safer with it in his hand.

"This one is," she said.

John watched the Hag rake through the mud and leaves which had started to compost.

Snarls surrounded them. Cold drops of rain hit the back of John's neck.

The Hag sniffed the air. Her nose twitched. A frown framed her face. "Do you smell sweet chili pepper?" She continued to crawl across the ground like a child searching for a toy.

John took a deep breath. Surprised by the smell of one of his favorite condiments. "Yeah. I do."

"Crap." She continued her search. Thunder roared in the distance. "Help me."

"Seriously?" John asked. He rushed over, blade in hand kicking up glistening wet leaves as he fumbled about. "You are going to get us eaten!" John stopped he could hear labored panting.

A short squat hodag had the black leather journal in its mouth. "I found your journal." He pointed the blade at the monster.

She scrambled forward towards the little beast. "Give that back." The hodag ran away from them instead.

A second came darting out of the woods intercepting him, taking the other side of the book as his prize. The two growled and snarled at each other, beginning a tug of war over the book.

"Let's go, that Journal is toast." John moved over to the woman and helped her off the ground. Her jacket shifted back exposing a long gash on her side covered in sticky blue gore.

"I need that back." She took the knife away from John and moved towards the fight. She plunged the blade into the smaller beast. The larger one still had the journal as he lolloped away towards John.

"Not more running." She moaned.

"A little help, please?" John said. He ran away from the larger hodag charging towards him.

"Lead it back this way," she said.

John's side ached. Spinning around, he ran back towards her.

The Hag crouched, blade in hand, bringing it down just after John passed. He turned around to see that she managed to pin the little nasty by the tail to the icy ground. She dropped to its level, trying to wrestle the journal out of its mouth. She succeeded and collapsed on the ground, journal clutched to her chest. The hodag took the opportunity to lick the blood leaking from her side. Her flesh sizzled and she howled in pain, smacking it away from her.

John scrambled for the knife, pulling the blade out of the creatures tail. John took the opportunity to try and stab the wriggling monster while the hodag was distracted by the oozing blood. He grunted as he pushed the blade through the hide, till the beast yipped in pain and died.

He pulled the monster off her. Part of the gore smearing across the back of his hand. "Yeowch!" He dropped the hodag on the ground.

"I appreciate not being eaten. I owe you one." She lay with her jacket splayed out underneath her. White shirt now stained blue.

"Yeah, you do." John helped her up and away from the fallen hodag.

The rest of the pack descended, feasting on the dead piece of flesh.

John's hand bubbled, he grimaced as pustules formed.

"I can fix that." The Hag held his wrist turning the hand over. She took the knife from John and slid it away.

"Wouldn't it be better if I hang onto that?" John asked. He liked that knife, it had good balance and felt sturdy, also an entrancing damascus pattern on the blade he had never seen before.

"No," she said. "We need to get moving. That snack won't take the pack long to eat."

The rain morphed to small flitting snowflakes. They made it to the parking lot where his navy sonata sat looking bedraggled and alone.

"You should have kept running," she said as John helped her along.

"Helping you seemed like a good idea at the time," He grunted, stepping over the curb into the parking lot.

A deep chortle came out of her and she winced. "Aw, that smarts! Where are we going anyway?"

"My car," John said. "And then to the Emergency Room."

"No cars or Emergency Rooms!" The woman stumbled back from the car and landed on her back side.

"Right, sure, let's get you to a hospital," John said. He hoisted her arm back over his shoulder.

"No." She clutched her side.

"Uh, yes," he said. He wrapped his arm around her waist trying to balance her weight.

She groaned. "And tell them what? A hodag ate a donor?"

John paused. "You need a patch up and I need to get my hand looked at." His hand sizzled, and fire pulsed up his forearm. His veins a sprawling road map of darkening green and purple.

"They won't be able to help you. You'll lose the hand." Her eyelids fluttered, as she seemed to fight with staying conscious.

"I need my hand," John said. "It's... handy."

The woman chortled. "Handy?"

"A hospital is my best bet." He looked down the flesh, now bruised purple and yellow radiated from the point of contact.

"Oh? Hospitals treat supernatural wounds?" She asked. She pulled the knife back out and waved it through the air.

"Can you fix this?" John asked. If he even wanted to consider being a surgeon, he needed both hands.

She nodded. "But no hospitals."

"Alright. Where are we going?"

"Your place." She grabbed his wrist, turned it palm down, and spat on his hand.

"Gross!" The slimy glob of phlegm spread over the wound,

sizzling as it soaked into his skin. A icy burst ran up his arm and into his chest.

The feeling retreated from his heart and down his arm. He sighed, at least it stopped hurting. "You spitting on me is still not the strangest thing to happen tonight." He took a breath, pulling in the cold night air. "I still think the hospital is the better choice."

"Hospitals ask questions. I don't like questions," her words began to slur together. "Your place." She pointed her blade towards the mountains. Her jacket fluttered exposing the bloody gash on her side. Every breath caused a crack to appear in it and leak blood. She touched it, "Huh, that'll leave a mark."

4

AN EAST WIND

Y ou sent hodags after her?" Zech asked. He leaned against a
tree, arms folded.

Hooded amber eyes squinted into the dark watching
the pack chase Lilith, and the poor sap she dragged along this time.
Really, he knew he was the only one that could keep her distracted.

Zech's shadow stretched out into the dark, lean and tall like the
trees around him. At least I'll be able to try again tomorrow. Zech
cherished the time he could get with Lilith even if it was only a
meal every few weeks.

He'd find a way to get the skull, didn't mean he couldn't take
his time making it happen. He'd been assigned by the powers that
be to get ahold of it. He just wished they hadn't made the
overzealous Gabe tag along.

"What do you think, dragon or fairy?" Gabe asked.

"Huh?" Zech tore his attention back to the other man.

"Did you not get a whiff of the boy? He's part corruption,
alright. I'm not sure what though," Gabe said. In the dark he
could've been confused for a boulder, large and craggy.

Unlike Zech his abilities were limited. When the abomination
corrupted the world, Gabe had been in the Legion only one day.

He could tell if something had supernatural genetics, but unlike full-fledged members, he couldn't tell what that heritage was.

He also trained obsessively with holy relics to make up for what he lacked.

Zech thought that it might all be part of his obsession with the Legion's mission to wipe out all traces of abomination in the world, regardless of how well they could kiss. Maybe Gabe might progress if they could undo what Lil had done.

None of them had wings. None of the troop could pass back and forth between this world and the other realms either, they were marooned in the mortal realm.

Zech smiled as Gabe took a step forward, with his weapon of choice. The Moringstar. Heavy rope and tied to the end, an ornate paddle about the length of his forearm. Curved slits were carved into the wood, thin fibers laced in the gaps and quivered in the air they whispered against in the night.

Gabe began spinning the weapon in front of him. It glowed a pale green, lighting up his face every time it passed. The whispers turned to bellows of thunder in the night.

Zech could see the sound waves forming a cacophonous orb, moving towards the pack, driving them forward into the trees.

Gabe caught the whirling noise maker in his hand, stopping the sound.

Zech took a deep breath, searching for a whiff of the boy. "Kid, might be part angel." A thin smile pulled across his lips. "Better have a chat with him. Where'd you get something for the hodags to track?"

"Your private stash of abomination memorabilia," Gabe smirked.

Zech bit his bottom lip, trying to dam a flood of memories of his past relationships with Lil. Letting himself slip into steamy recollections wasn't the best plan just now. He didn't have too many momentos left. Though he should have done a better job hiding them. He hated that he'd been used to cause her pain. Lilith could handle it, but he didn't want to be a part of the cause.

"Don't worry, Lilith will survive passing through the digestive tract of a hodag." Gabe watched the boy tumble down a hill after Lilith. "Don't know about the boy."

"Call'em off then." Zech narrowed his eyes. The boy and Lilith rolled from sight. He should be the only one tumbling down a hill with her, clothing optional. He tugged at the reigns of his imagination, zeroing in on the present moment. "If that kid is a mix, he could be useful." Zech took a couple of steps forward to help, eager to get some space between Lilith and the boy.

"No, you know the rules." Gabe's brow furrowed.

Zech frowned and recited in a dead-pan voice, "No contact with the abomination."

Gabe held the thick rope in his hand and snapped it. "But, maybe the boy could be of use." He rested the rope over the back of his neck. "Are you picking up anything off the kid?"

"Not close enough," Zech took a step.

Gabe held up his arm, blocking his path. "Let's clean up first." He rubbed his palms together and white sparks crackled along the length of the rope. He stretched the rope above his head twisted light engulfed it, then brought it down on the ground in front of him. A loud crack of thunder rippled through the air.

Zech clapped his hands over his ears. "Give a guy a little warning."

Gabe laughed, his thick meaty hands tightened around the rope. "I love that sound."

Icy rain slipped down the neck of Zech's black hoodie. Shivering, he pulled the hood up. "Can you quit it with the water-works."

"All part of the fun, Lover-boy," Gabe looked up to the sky as the slush turned to rain.

"Allegedly." Zech tried not to think of the last time they had been together.

Mental images of her sprawled out across his bed, cold morning light spilling over her bare back. He bit his lip again, driving the memory back down before all the colors and smells of her eclipsed his desire to step away from them.

Zech may have a higher rank than Gabe, but his involvement with Lil meant his superiors kept an eye on him.

Zech reluctantly pulled his own blade out from the palm of his hand. An advantage of being a full fledge member of the legion. His skin sizzled as he brought out the weapon, not quite pain, but close. He could feel the flow of energy come from within and fill the blade. Gabe's rope, while great for large sweeping waves of destruction, was not a weapon for detail work. Zech's blade provided precision and finesse, something he felt the boorish angel lacked.

"I don't like letting her get away." Gabe dug his heel in to the damp ground prepping to storm the pack.

"She's taken quite the beating tonight. She'll die, and you can sniff her out." Zech gave the blade a few test swings, raindrops sizzling on the bright white-hot blade.

"Hodags, first. Abomination, next," Gabe all but salivated as he spoke.

"I still think we should try asking her for help," Zech said.

"How many times have we killed her? No one has been able to reason with her." Gabe said.

"I sort of did," Zech said. He swung the blade at the ground opening a large gash that filled with mud and slush.

"Allegedly." Gabe smirked.

Zech ignored him, "Are they clear?"

"Yes."

Zech started walking towards the pack. "Let's go then."

Zech took to slashing and dicing hodags. Emerald goo streamed and hissed through the air as he worked out his frustrations on the little beasts. The mess looked like a Jackson Pollock painting. *If Cheri would let me spend some time with Lilith I could get this sorted.* The head of the legions didn't see the point of talking to what she deemed as the epitome of all sin and transgression. The abomination, source of all corruption, as Gabe was so fond of saying was still dear to his heart, or at least familiar to his bed.

Gabe hit the ground, the rope enlarged and now, looked as if it could be used to anchor a cargo ship.

Hodags flew into the air and tumbled across the ground. Another round of thunder rolled out into the valley. "You say something?"

"No." Zech rammed the blade through the skull of a still twitching critter.

"One less pack." Gabe looked up and growled. Lilith was gone. "May not have been able to grab the abomination but at least the night isn't a total waste."

"We'll find her." Zech sniffed the air. The sulfuric smell of hodag burned his nostrils. He started to follow them.

"Hold on, Cheri won't like it if we leave traces of hodags. We have a mess to clean up." Gabe said pointing back towards the Plasma Center.

"Why'd you have to bring in hodags, anyway?" Zech asked.

"Good trackers and easy to exterminate. Serves a two-fold mission. Which two parts Zech?"

"Capture the abomination and exterminate the rot she brought into the world," Zech sighed through the words he understood but didn't really have his heart behind.

"And what is an abomination?" Gabe asked, playing the teacher, which he wasn't.

"Anything that lives longer than a standard mortal life is an abomination," Zech said and rolled his eyes. "Are there students here that I missed? Or did you forget that I am the one with higher rank?"

Gabe plowed forward without listening. "That is the legion's purpose." Gabe crossed his arms looking over the carnage and smiled. The hodags bodies began to melt and blend into the ground.

Zech, kicked a pile of damp leaves, "Fine."

"Come on, then," Gabe said. He rolled up the rope rubbing the palms of his hands together with a crackle the light, disappeared.

Zech smiled. "Race ya." He zipped ahead. Another advantage, if he could see where he was trying to go and focus on that point, he could be there in a moment. No one in the legions moved as quick as he did. He wanted to see the carnage the hodags had made at the plasma center without Gabe's preaching about abominations and holy duty.

He traced the trail of destruction back to the center, arriving at the emergency exit. He knocked on the glass, causing a pudgy guy, hidden beneath the table to jump and knock his head.

A thin wisp of a woman came and opened the door to the break room wrinkles marred her face, and pale brown eyes stared him down. She tucked a loose strand of flaxen hair back up into her bun. "May I help you?"

Zech could smell lemon zest and copper coming off the woman. She reeked of fairy. Better keep an eye on her. While everyone else backed away from the door, she acted as if she was about to invite him in for tea.

He stood up straight and pulled out his wallet. He flipped it open and snapped it shut. No one really checked his credentials if Lilith had been around. "Yes, I'm detective Michaels. We received a call about an incident."

The woman's thoughts drifted into Zech's mind. *Finally, I won't have to listen to Mark whine anymore.*

Zech smiled. He may not be able to date who he liked but being the leader of the squadron had perks, like being able to hear the thoughts of those around him.

"Oh, John must've called. That's very good of him. I'm Iris." The thin woman extended a wrinkled hand.

Zech avoided shaking her hand. "May I come in?"

"Please!" That had come from the blob of a man under the table, whose bottom lip quivered like green jello.

"Mark. You need to take a moment." Iris stepped out of Zech's way letting him into the building. She continued talking to him. "You'll have to excuse him. Doesn't have the strongest constitution. Thinks he can get out of cleaning the mess up if he pouts."

Zech stifled a laugh. "Iris, would you mind taking me through what happened?"

"I'll show you. Whatever it was, is gone now." She led him out into the center.

A glorious mess sprawled through the center. Chewed medical

tape hung like streamers across the bays. Machines toppled, and the ceiling fractured. Zech assumed from the fallen ventilation hood that was how the Hodags broke in. Yep. Lilith was here.

"I'm the only one that has been out of the break room yet. Everyone else is too scared to leave." Iris flattened a crease in her lab coat.

Zech nodded. "I'll gather some statements and get them moving home."

"Not looking forward to dealing with this mess though." Iris nose twitched. She straightened her collar.

"Can you give me an idea of how this happened?"

Best not to mention my landlady was here. She was covered in horse feces no less. Shameful. Iris placed a finger on her chin. "I didn't see anything myself, but John, the manager on duty, asked me to clear everyone out. I assume a disgruntled donor. Though why they'd do so much damage is beyond me." Iris kicked a chewed plasma bottle under a table. No need to mention hodags.

Zech smiled. Find John, and he'd find Lilith.

Bonus, Iris lived on a property owned by Lilith, one of her stashes perhaps? Zech stepped around the mess, admiring the carnage. Never boring with Lilith around.

His mind wandered again, this time to Pompeii. Lilith looked breathtaking in a pale violet toga standing on the jagged lip of the mouth of the volcano. He could still feel the heat that rushed out with every page she threw in.

Determined to be done with him, for what felt like the hundredth time. Every page she fed Vesuvius caused it to rumble and churn. The magic in those pages fed the rage of the volcano and caused the doom of Pompeii.

When she learned this wasn't the first time they had been together, or the second, or third for that matter, things stopped being sultry. He'd lied to her and she intended to erase him. She was willing to cause a natural disaster to make it happen. By removing pages from the journal, the magic that bound them caused tears in the world, he'd seen her do it before then. Natural disasters, economic depressions, mankind suffered if she destroyed those pages and when the pages were gone, so were her memories. Still he couldn't stop her, not when she looked so amazing in the morning light.

The break ups were never his fault. Lil would accuse him of lying. He'd never lie, as an angel he couldn't, didn't mean he hadn't learn to become creative with the truth, and leaving history out was exactly what she was doing, so he thought of it more like giving her what she wanted.

Lilith always over-reacted, a real flare for the dramatic, at Pompeii she had thrown herself in with the last page. Zech ran his hand over a scar on the inside of his upper arm. He'd been blessed to live. The raised scar from pulling her from the lava, reminded him he'd find a way to make it work.

However, Lilith removing her memories gave him a chance to try again, as many times as he saw fit. Maybe one day, he'd get it right and she'd at least bother to keep a line or two about him on the page. He wanted more, but at the moment he'd take any rcollection.

Iris's thoughts interrupted him. Bit of an odd one. She raised a brow. "Are you alright there?"

"Damage assessment. I'll have to take some extensive pictures see if the potential for repeat attacks is possible."

Iris nodded. With Cailleach? I could guarantee it.

Zech tried not to laugh. Cailleach was a term the fairy clans used for Lilith. Old hag wasn't a unfair description after some of her dealings with the fae. He cleared his throat. "I think I have a solution for your mess. I know a stellar cleanup crew. The state will even foot the bill." He could put Gabe on it while he waited for Lilith to start to stink. She reeked when she healed and from the looks of it, she didn't walk away unscathed.

If Gabe was busy cleaning, the big lug would be out of his way for a while.

Iris clasped her hands in front of her chest. "Wonderful! Anything else Detective? After all the excitement, I'd like to get home and put my feet up. Maybe even drink a cup of tea."

Zech pulled out a notepad. "I'll need your full Name, way to contact you, and your current address for my report. I'll pass by to follow up."

5

ROTTEN BACON

John dragged the woman out of the orchard. Her arm over his shoulder and his hand wrapped around her waist. He kept looking behind him, expecting the swarm to come and finish them off. The skies stopped crying, *What's with this weather? Even this isn't normal for Utah.*

A white flash silhouetted the trees, then silence. *Was that lightning?* Thunder rippled out after the light.

John's hand shook, everything made him jump.

He huffed as he fumbled with his car keys, trying to balance the dead weight on his shoulder. It wasn't working. Giving up, he rested the woman against the back door of his car, opening the front door, he slid her into the car where she thumped onto the seat. When he pulled back, his hands were covered in dark blue viscous liquid.

The light is messing with me. Blood is red, not blue. He tried to wipe it off but it clung to his hands like dried school glue. Curiosity pushed down the fear. *That's different.*

John slammed the door shut, walked around the car, and got in. He started the car. He stared at the woman conked out in the seat next to him. His hand no longer hurt, but a silver shine took over where the green hodag blood had sizzled his flesh. She kept her word and healed his hand.

"I should take you to the hospital." John's fingers drummed on the gray vinyl of his steering wheel. The hag, for lack of a better name, didn't belong at a hospital. Her tattered jacket revealed the cut on her arm. A thin silvery line interrupted a patchwork of tattoos, like a snake slithering through tall grass.

She kept her word, he would keep his. The engine of the car turned over and John headed to his place. He knew enough to keep her alive. He hoped.

John pulled up to his apartment. The white paneling of the building in stark contrast with the dark night sky.

He parked and turned off the car.

Exhaustion had leaked into his bones. He got out and went to the passenger-side opening the door. "Hey?" he shook her shoulder.

She grunted in response.

"At least you're not dead."

Like a bag of Idaho potatoes she tumbled out, landing on the pavement with a thud.

John sighed. He hooked his arms under her shoulders and dragged her to the stairs. He hauled her up one stair at a time, a resounding thump as her butt hit each one.

His back hurt. John sighed this was not how he wanted to spend his night.

At the top of the stairs, he leaned her in the doorway, while he fished his keys out of his pocket. They jangled as he unlocked the door. The woman started to slide down the door frame. John caught her as his butt knocked the front door open.

Listening for the sound of Sarah, he as always hoped she'd be there. He gave her a key and he wished she'd use it more often.

The fridge hummed in the corner.

He sighed. No Sarah.

It would've been helpful to have another set of hands. John again hooked his arms under the armpits of the woman dragging her into his studio apartment. He tripped over his gym shorts and stumbled again over a dirty shirt. Shifting his grip, trying to get a better hold on her. The woman's knife clattered out of its sheath and onto the wood floor, next to a pile of empty moving boxes.

John wished Sarah would move in already and save herself some money and the stress of her semi-crazed roommate. There was something wrong with Sarah, that she'd rather live with crazy than him.

He pulled back a disheveled navy-blue comforter, it smelt of lavender and vanilla. Sarah's body wash. John grimaced, the beautiful fragrance was about to be obliterated by the awful stench that drifted off the body on his floor.

He retrieved the woman and heaved her on the bed. The gash stopped oozing. He scrambled for the first aid kit in the bathroom, just in case it reopened.

The standard white bathroom was nothing special though it had a full tub. Bits of color managed to sneak into the room, the gray grout in the tile, the dark brown wood of the bathroom vanity, and the silver faucet. Scrounging beneath the bathroom sink, John found the first aid kit. Sarah promised to consider moving in if he could keep the bathroom clean for a month. She'd probably have a new challenge thought up when time ran out. He'd scrub the bathroom a thousand times more if it meant he kept her in his life. She challenged him and it didn't hurt that she had legs for days. She was simple happiness. Nothing felt so hopeless or difficult when she was there.

He grabbed the kit and headed back to the bed. The bleeding stopped, nothing but dark, thick, crusty blue blood was left. It looked like hardened rock candy.

The wound across her side and stomach began to bubble. *What the hell!* John stumbled back a little, tripping over the dirty shirt and landing on his butt. The long gash down her side boiled. Pustules formed, swirling around the gash like hot butter stirred in a frying pan.

John could feel his own pulse throbbing in his neck, his blood racing to return to his heart. He'd seen wounds before, but normally when you cut something, it didn't start to melt.

He pulled himself back up crawling towards the bed something smelled like rotten bacon being seared. He gagged, covering his mouth and nose. John ran over to the window and threw it open before edging back towards the bed. He watched in shocked horror-fascination as the gray flesh knit itself back together. A long thin scar appeared, trailing up her side.

John rubbed his eyes and looked again. The wound now looked like a knot on an old oak tree. Not that the night needed to get any weirder but the woman continued to surprise him. The scar on her flesh translucent and gnarled.

Then what sounded like bark cracking filled the room, the blood on her skin breaking into pieces. A kaleidoscope of blue shifted and moved revealing gray skin as some of the blood seeped back into her body through the pores of her skin.

"What are you?" John asked the unconscious woman sprawled out on his bed. A snort came out of her and then her chest rose and fell like gentle waves.

The few traces of blood left on her skin, from where the jacket contained the mess, flaked off on to the sheets. John looked down at his hands, covered in blue gore from helping her into the car. He stretched his hand, the blood still held on like a plastic glove. A pungent smell wafted from her body.

He moved closer and stretched his hand out in front of him, placing it on her belly. He felt the blood tighten, then harden.

He pulled his hand away leaving a blue hand print on the skin of her stomach. It cracked and seeped in just like before. John looked at his hand, clear of any remaining gore, and then back at her stomach, nothing.

"That's so cool." He pulled a deep breath in, "But, different." John pressed his other hand to her, then picked bits off the coat, dropping them on the body like a child throwing rocks in the river, each piece disappearing. "How?" Some of the blood pooled rolling on the sheets like marbles.

John needed a moment. He backed away and ran into the bathroom. He shut the door and turned the lock with a click. Yanking open the drawer on the vanity to block the door, He fumbled with the cabinet doors, pulling out a six pack of toilet paper from under the sink. Pilling it in front of the door as a barricade, he stood up. *That really won't do much will it?*

John caught a whiff of himself, dirt, manure, and something else. Clean clothes and a shower would help. John blustered, surveying the damage done to his body. A scrape ached on his hand. His lower back throbbed. He pulled off his tattered lab coat, mud had soaked the bottom. A gradient of dark-brown to off-red stretched up from the hem.

"Great." He muttered. His jeans now exposed his knee and his light blue button down shirt was beyond repair, the strange blue line intermingled with the plasma stain. John hated clothes shopping. He yanked off his shirt, the last remaining buttons popped off. On the top of his shoulder some pale itchy scaling from his psoriasis seemed to pulse red.

"Perfect. A flare up." He scratched at the loose skin, peeling flakes off and throwing them in the trash can. He finished undressing and got in the shower. Stepping under the water, he washed the day away, gave himself a good scrub, and turned off the water. Stepping out, he grabbed a threadbare towel, wrapping it around his hips.

He removed the useless barrier, he set up in front of the door and opened it a crack.

The woman hadn't moved. He crept out, heading for the closet. John liked living alone, he could wear as much or as little as he liked and hoped Sarah did the same when she lived with him.

The woman muttered something unintelligible, as he passed. She flopped around trying to free herself of her jacket.

"Oh, Good Grief." John moved closer and pulled it out from beneath her, the stained blouse came off with it. He averted his eyes and threw the items on the floor. John considered leaving the gloves, but who sleeps with gloves on? He pulled them off. One hand was covered in deep scars that looked like burn marks. They were bubbled and warped like fungus on a tree trunk. Removing the other glove revealed a hand covered with long scratches like aged bark.

He rolled up the gloves and put them in the pocket of the

jacket on the floor. His fingers glanced over the leather journal inside. *What's in here worth getting killed over?* He pulled out the book, his skin prickled and he shuddered.

Something about the book was wrong, left him feeling slimy like the smell of rotting bacon had.

He dropped it back on the coat, like a hot coal. John turned back to the stranger on his bed.

She could sleep with her boots on. At least until he put pants on.

Her arms were a patchwork of scars and tattoos. Giant serpents wrapped her arms trying to eat symbols John had never seen before. A visual maze of scales and claws. He shuddered and pulled the covers over her making the monsters disappear. John turned away and rubbed his face.

The hag flailed behind him, thumping the mattress. John turned back, the blue serpent glared at him from her arm. She kicked off all the sheets like a child and lay there half-naked in her splattered blue jeans.

John looked at the ceiling and pulled the sheet over her again.

If Sarah did come in, he didn't want her to walk in on a half-naked woman on his bed. *Maybe this wasn't the best idea.* What kind of danger had he invited in? He yawned and checked his phone.

Sarah normally called when she got in for the night. He sent her a quick message. "You won't believe the night I've had. Talk to you soon. Love You." He waited, no answer. He frowned, the apartment felt empty despite his current company.

"Zech." The woman spoke in her sleep. Then incoherent babbling spewed out a mess of syllables and sounds he couldn't understand.

"Zech?" Sounds biblical. John rubbed his chin. Short red stubble caught at his fingers. Sarah didn't like his beard, so he shaved it. He'd rather have kisses than a beard anyway. He headed back to the bathroom turning the tap on, hot water steamed from the sink he prepared to shave.

In the morning, he'd give the woman a ride home, go take his biology test and have dinner with Sarah. The shaving cream hissed as it came out of the aerosol can. Menthol drifted up his nostrils and his skin tingled. The razor pulled against his skin. It'd be time for a new razor soon. This one might last another week. He paused half his face still covered in shaving cream. "My textbook." He left it on the desk before the attack. Work. Crap. When he left, the textbooks all seemed safe, but work was a complete mess.

"It could be worse." John ran the razor over his face again, the steam rising from the sink.

6

IS THAT BODY PAINT?

S arah sighed, the key to John's place heavy in her hand. *Tonight. I'll end it tonight.* She chanted this line over and over again as she marched up the stairs.

Pushing a long blonde lock behind her ear, she kept up her chant. Her roommate Lisa might go mad if she complained about John again.

When they first meet he'd been something new and interesting. She'd been in Minnesota over the summer, touring the U of M campus. He was a med student who volunteered to lead tours to visiting and new students. Of all the tour guides, he was the cutest, in his own dorky way.

She never thought he'd change schools for her, let alone move across the country. Sarah had to think about the future and what a life with John would look like. She didn't like the idea of living through lean times while he got his degrees. Quiet nights sitting around while he studied didn't appeal. John loved to talk about 'their' dream house and how many kids they'd have. He never noticed that she never added to those conversations. John tended to linger like a song that caught in your head and never left. *He can be so sweet, but I've no patience for clingy.*

The dark blue door loomed in front of her. She checked her

phone, ignoring the unread message from him. She could send him a text, end it that way.

Coward. She chastised herself.

Some things should be said in person. She dropped the phone in her pocket but reconsidered the text option. She straightened her pale blue blouse, pulling her black woolen coat closer over petite shoulders.

She took a breath and pictured John at his desk pouring over circulatory systems. She'd walk in and just tell him it's over, place the key on his desk, and leave. Simple. He'd probably cry, but he could find someone else to smother. She'd go grab ice cream with Lisa and celebrate her new-found freedom.

Her pale fingers gripped the key, feeling like they belonged to someone else. The key scraped in the lock as she turned the doorknob. A familiar sound that used to make her smile, now it filled her with dread.

The chair at the desk did not hold John. He stood in a towel in the bathroom doorway. His hair damp and droplets of water clinging to his skin. Her eyes traced his shoulders like her fingers often had. She liked his shoulders, though he called them weak. Her gaze tracked over his chest but, stopped as she noticed the shock spreading across his face.

Her gaze landing on the occupied bed. A strange woman sprawled across the bed, her joints at strange angles. On the floor, a tattered shirt and red coat splattered in blue, light streaks of that same color were on her bare skin. She looked as if she had been pulled from a penny dreadful story.

Sarah couldn't stand horror. John loved it.

Sarah blinked, her head cocked to the side, and her lips pursed. Anger bubbled in her stomach. *What the hell is this?*

"I can explain." John held his towel up to keep it from slipping further down his hips, as he walked towards her.

Rage bubbled in the place the dread had been. She pulled it all inside. She would use it to lambaste him in a moment. Her molars ground together as she took a deep breath in through her nose. She held up a hand and he halted in place. "Your sexual partners are none of my concern." She marched over to the bed running her finger through the blue goo caught on the sheets. She glowered at the sticky blue substance on the tip of her index finger. *Latex? Body paint?* She rubbed the goo between her fingers and gave it a sniff. Sweet summer fruits drifted up from the substance. "Smells great." She spat the words out letting her rage seep out. "What is this anyway?"

"It's not what you think," John said.

Sarah cut him off. "Oh, what should I think it is? Smells edible, and she is coated in it." She licked her finger, the sickly sweet flavor of blueberries trickled across her tongue. "Yep, even tastes tacky."

A gurgle came out of the woman.

John's face contorted in disgust.

"What? You're allowed to lick edible body paint off someone and I'm not even allowed to taste it?" *She looks like a tramp.* On the gray sheets, another small blue glob sat. "Is it blueberry or raspberry? I can't tell." She picked up another piece and swallowed it down.

The woman shifted exposing more skin. Strange scars ran up her side. Parts of her back covered in strange etchings and tattoos that crested up and over her hip bones, all the backs of scaled creatures. "You cheated on me, for this?" Sarah waved a hand over the still sleeping figure.

"No. Let me get some clothes on and I'll explain—"

"Give you a chance to lie? You can't explain away a partially nude woman covered in body paint in your bed." Sarah's eyes began to sting. Tears tumbled down her face escaping down her cheeks. *I'm such an idiot, of course he cheated on me.*

John's jaw dropped. "She needed help!"

"And you thought a tumble in the sheets would cure what ails her?"

"No!"

Sarah crossed her arms over her chest, her head began to slowly bob up and down. *I need to get out of here.*

The woman snorted and grabbed for a pillow. Sarah's pillow. Her nostrils flared.

John moved toward the bed.

"You know what, she can have my pillow, and you for that matter." She slapped the key down on the desk and headed for the door.

"Hold on." John grabbed her by the arm before she could leave. Sarah broke her arm free and snarled.

"I don't even know her name," John said. He waved at the body on the bed. The towel slipped and fell to the floor. John gasped. He let go of her arm and grabbed the towel off the floor.

Sarah felt her chest constrict. Even naked she wanted, no needed, to hurt him. She glanced down at the towel. "At least you've found someone you can finally please in bed." She pulled the door open and escaped.

She fled down the steps and back towards her car. She dialed Lisa, then turned the car and squealed out of the parking lot by the second ring. Before her roommate could speak, Sarah took control of the conversation. "I hate when you're right."

Lisa warned her that John may be hiding things from her. She always seemed to be able to figure people out pretty quick.

"What happened?" Lisa asked, concern painted her voice.

Sarah sighed. "Half-naked woman covered in blue body paint." She took a breath. "In John's bed. Added bonus, naked John and the body paint was edible." Sarah sobbed a little then laughed. "If not, I'm in trouble."

"How would you know that?" Lisa asked. "Did you join them?" Amusement ringed in her voice.

"No." Sarah shook her head, berating herself for being so rash. "I ate some."

"Off of the body?"

"No! A clump of it from the gray sheets. I loved those sheets." Lisa had the phone on speaker as she drove down the road.

"The ones I helped you buy?" Lisa asked.

"Yes!" Sarah headed towards the house off Seventh West.

"Bastard." Lisa's tone turned harsh.

"Yep." Sarah sniffled again.

"Where are you?"

"The road to our house, passing work."

"I'm sitting outside. Why did you eat it?" Lisa asked.

"Because I could." Sarah pulled into her driveway and parked.

"Uh, huh. Why?" she asked again. Lisa slipped out of the shadows, ending the call. She wore dirty denim and a bright red shirt. Raven hair braided in a single plait hung over her shoulder. Her skin the tone of topaz when lit by the sun.

Sarah rolled her eyes as Lisa got in the car. "I, wanted to make John pay."

Lisa put her arm around Sarah. "You've done one better, he'll think you're insane," Lisa said. Her deep brown, almond shaped eyes lit up.

"That's not a good thing." She sniffled, wiping the tears away with the back of her hand.

"Yes, it is. Will he try to get back together with someone unstable?"

"No."

"Then if eating a little bit of used body paint is all it took to get rid of a clingy boyfriend, good job."

Sarah laughed and hugged Lisa back. "Lisa, you're the best."

"Ice cream?" she asked buckling her seat belt.

"Yes. Can we walk?" Sarah said.

"Fine." Lisa sighed, undoing her seat belt. The women got out of the car and headed down Ninth North passing the local Costco and turning onto State Street. They walked in silence until they paused at a light. "How far are we going?" Lisa asked.

"Macey's It's not that far." Sarah sniffled, wiping away lingering tears.

"I thought John would be the one crying." Lisa smiled.

"Break ups still suck." Sarah checked her phone, deleting the unread text.

"Yep."

The two women headed towards the local grocery store, past the gas station, and The Lehi Roller Mill. Together they walked through the sliding doors and headed for the freezer section.

"I didn't think John had it in him to cheat." Lisa mused pulling open the freezer, cool air spilling out. She held up a tub of double chocolate brownie.

Sarah nodded yes.

"Yikes, we are hitting the hard stuff tonight." Lisa mused. "Funny, considering how much you complain about how vanilla he behaved." Lisa smiled and pulled a second tub out for herself. "Do we need to go find something a little stronger?"

"No. I don't feel like beer, and the closest State Liquor Store will be closed by the time we get there."

"Might do you some good to go out." Lisa closed the freezer door.

"I don't feel like it. Where do you even get blue body paint?" Sarah threw her arms up in the air. As she walked back up to the top of the aisles.

"There is that one store on Main St. or Amazon." Lisa said as she followed her. They headed towards the checkout and opted for the self-checkout machine and paid. "This is really getting to you."

Sarah frowned, her brow furrowed. *I wanted to break up with him.*

"But I get it, you've never been good at sharing your toys," Lisa said. She placed the frosty pints into the plastic bag.

"It's John, he's not exactly the sexiest guy on the face of the planet," Sarah picked up the bag.

"Just because you don't want him anymore, doesn't mean no one else is interested." Lisa started walking towards the exit.

One of Sarah's coworkers walked in the automatic doors pushing a cart. "Hello, girls," Iris said. She stopped and stared at Sarah, the smile dropping from her face. She let go of the shopping cart and huffed in a deep breath. Floating towards Sarah like a moth caught in the light of a bug zapper. The smell of rust and lemon floated off the old woman. Sarah stepped back. Nausea roiled her stomach as the woman came closer.

Iris shook her head, grabbed her cart and disappeared into the produce aisle.

"Strange." Lisa folded henna-toned arms across her chest.

Sarah shrugged, then shuddered. As they walked out the doors, she crashed into a giant of a man. Falling on her backside, she yelped.

Lisa helped Sarah up and turned to stare down the assailant.

"Hey, what's the big idea?" Lisa asked, hands on hips.

The guy shrugged, he towered over her by a full head. His eyes boring into Lisa.

Without warning, a meaty hand grabbed at a black pendant near her chest. "Where did you get that?" he asked.

Lisa stepped back pivoting away to get some distance between them.

"None of your business." Lisa dropped the pendant down her shirt.

"Let's go." Sarah grabbed Lisa's hand, pulling her away.

The girls ran up the sidewalk and back past the Roller Mill. Lisa pulled her around the corner of the white brick, hiding them from sight.

Sarah peeked around the corner, no sign of the guy. "Weirdo," Sarah said.

"I could've handled him," Lisa said. She pulled the necklace out from her shirt, rubbing the deep black stone.

"Uh-huh, sure." Sarah shook her head, *I'm the insane one?*

Thunder passed above them, like a freight train passing, in a clear sky.

Together they walked back up the road. Sarah kept looking over her shoulder while Lisa seemed unruffled after the stranger tried to grab her.

"Are you okay?" Lisa asked.

"I should be asking you that." Sarah put her hands in the pockets of her coat.

Lisa shrugged. "No harm done."

Sarah shuddered, between the gross scene she had walked in at John's, Iris's bizarro behavior, and the weirdo making a grab for Lisa, the whole world felt like it turned on a different axis. Nothing else could go wrong, right?

7

NOT MY KIN

Iris sighed, easing into her maroon wing-chair tipped with bronze upholstery tacks. The modest living room with pale blue shag carpet, white walls, and a large window overlooked the front yard. An old oak filled the yard blocking some of the noise of the busy road beyond it. The last remaining orchard spread up the hill, they used to spread for miles.

Now a good portion of the land had been turned into developments houses all squished together. *To many people and not enough land,* Iris thought to herself. She missed traveling the world with the other fairy clans, and a world not swarming with people. At least the farmhouse property remained the same. The property protected Callieach's secrets, all locked away deep below the roots of the oak tree.

A gruff voice from the heating duct interrupted her thoughts. Her son, Connor. "How on earth did a human get the hag's blood?"

"I'm as puzzled as you are, dear," Iris said.

Connor still maintained his true form and now led the clan. She had grown used to the array of voices that came from the ducts, walls, and occasionally the sinks. The only interactions she could manage with the family she could never see again. She wondered whether or not they were real. But the constant chatter proved otherwise.

She held on to her memories of what they looked like, but the images of her son and family were falling away like autumn leaves.

Her son would repeat stories she forgot from when she led the clan. Whether they were true or not, they amused her and passed the hours when she wasn't at work.

She took a sip of the hot lemon tea, savoring the undertones of rose hips.

"We should do something about that," Connor said.

"Connor, you will do nothing. I will do something." Iris's back ached. "Blasted contract."

"You alright, Mum?"

"Being human is terrible, dear."

"Worse than death?" The voice of Agnes, Connor's wife (or mate) joined the conversation. The original contract with Cailleach had a time limit. Iris broke the deal by trying to kill The Hag. For breaking the agreement, the head of the clan took responsibility. Iris lost her true form and became human, and The Hag would've probably eaten Iris if Connor hadn't brokered a new deal.

Connor and Agnes continued to bicker in the vent. "Cailleach's wind, Agnes. How long will you hold that over me?" Connor asked Agnes.

"When the acorn grows into a tree and you make me a casket." Agnes said. The vent rattled as if someone kicked the duct wall.

"You think I'd let my mother be eaten by The Hag?" Connor asked. Another scuffle and the noise from the duct stopped.

"If The Hag could stomach her, she'd have broken her end of the deal. We'd be a free clan." Agnes blamed Iris for everything that bothered her.

"No one sets us free through death. We'd have always been beholden to her memory." Connor always reminded her that the new contract with The Hag was her fault. Iris sighed. *I didn't want to be saved, foolish child.*

The tea cup clinked on the saucer as she put it down. "Have you ever considered what would have happened if I had died?"

"Tears and trouble," Connor said.

Iris shook her head. "Freedom. I'd be loose to the skies and the clan could've roamed again. Found the others."

"Something we can agree on," Agnes added, acidic grief in her voice.

Agnes had not been Iris's first choice for her son, or second, or third. *I should've told him no as a child.* But despite her lack of tact, Agnes made up for it in smarts.

"Our own come first." Connor yelled up from below. The grate shuddered. "You make The Hag seem like some awful larger than life legend. When all she really is a human gone strange."

Iris pursed her lips. The first contract kept them all safe from the holy terrors that descended from above. But it had a time limit. The deal Connor struck didn't.

"You could tell The Hag that a human is running around with a bit of her blood," Agnes said.

"That I could, or if I get hold of it, there may be something I could bargain for." Iris said. She took another sip of tea.

"No, absolutely not. I don't like your bargains," Connor said.

"You'd have to be quick. The Hag should've already noticed her blood is missing." Agnes seemed to be coming around to her way of thinking. They could hold the blood ransom for something useful.

"Not if she has new skin for her journals to distract her." Iris smiled inhaling the zesty lemon. "She's been running low, right?"

"Yes, she is. New skin. Now that is something," Connor mused.

"I've been keeping an eye on this one. He's part faerie. He could be turned against her. Twice the use and double the worth," Iris watched the bits of remaining tea leaves swirl and twist in the bottom of her cup. She could see change coming. Would the boy be useful?

"When do we meet him?" Agnes asked.

"Hopefully you don't," Iris said. She turned the cup upside down on the saucer.

"I don't wish what's below this house on anyone," Connor said.

"No one does." Agnes sighed.

"Then, don't speak to this one," Iris said. She picked up the cup. She couldn't make sense of the pattern of the leaves.

"What do you see?" Connor asked.

Iris shook her head and yawned. "Leaves."

"Are you sure you don't need our help?" Agnes asked.

"I'll be able to manage to get a bit of blood."

"I sometimes wonder if The Hag let you keep a bit of magic. Night, Iris." Agnes' small steps clinked in the vent as she took off.

She stood up, picking up the cup and saucer, and heading to the kitchen, rinsing the items off in the deep white sink, while a vent blasted cold air on her feet.

"I'd feel better if you took someone with you," Connor said from the vent near her feet.

"You're always looking for a way out. You leave and she'll know. Then, I'll be short a bargaining chip," Iris said. She looked out the big window above the kitchen sink, a line of pines blocked the shops down the road while stars began to take their place in the night sky.

"But—"

Iris placed the cup and saucer on a tea towel. "Don't stand in the vent if the air is blowing, you'll catch cold." She glared at the vintage grate.

"Alright, alright. Should I prep a room for our guest?"

Iris's head moved back and forth like a slow metronome as she considered the thought. "Just in case. May not use it. I don't know if anyone will miss the girl."

"I'd recommend it. With The Hag in town, there will be enough attention drawn to this place."

Iris nodded. "Maybe that's what we need, more attention, not less. She won't stick around if she starts receiving unwanted advances."

"No, I don't want any of the clan being 'cleansed' because you think it may get rid of The Hag for a few years. All things considered, The Hag has never broken her word with us. Although on many occasions, it'd be in her right to set some of your antics straight." The vent rattled.

Crows-feet deepened on Iris's face as she smiled. Between the blood, the girl, and the boy she would have all she needed to distract The Hag. Allowing her a chance to get down into the catacombs she called a library and find the contract. "My concern is your freedom. If I can, I'll stab the hag with a borrowed knife."

8

THE MORNING BREAKS

Hunger gnawed at Lilith's gut when she woke, her stomach gurgled in protest. A jolt of pain up her side reminded her of last night's near miss, her fatal fall, and consumed heart. She sat up, but John was nowhere to be seen in the studio apartment.

At least she hadn't died a third time. Vague memories floated to the surface of her mind. Still, better than waking up with no idea what happened surrounded by dead bodies.

She'd be feeling all of these injuries for weeks. She healed quick enough but the pain lingered. Her leg throbbed, three cracked ribs flared with every breath, fiery pain where her gut knitted back together, and a dull ache resonated in her heart with every beat.

Food. Food would ease the throbbing. If she ate she could ignore them.

She rubbed her head. *I better write John down before I forget.* She reached for her jacket on the floor, *What happened?* The red coat looked like a wounded animal trying to crawl away. She picked it up, pulled out her journal, then searched for a pen. *I've lost my pen. I liked that pen.* Lilith leaned over the side of the bed looking underneath at a land of odds and ends.

She spotted something glinting in the dark. "That better be my pen," She flopped off the bed, hand fumbling over clothes, a set of weights, and something squishy. "Victory!" she pulled out the pen from beneath the bed. Opening the journal, she scrawled some quick notes of last night's events. Her stomach growled for her to hurry up and be done. She finished up, shook her hand out, and put the journal down on the bed.

Her skin prickled, the room chilled.

She winced at the light that cut through the blinds. Something sweet permeated the air, like fresh donuts. Her skin itched and her eye twitched. She licked her fingers. Her nose twitched the smell came from her coat.

Damn it. I love this jacket. She licked the fabric and began tearing it into strips. She bit chunks off like jerky, except seasoned with plasma. Her body metabolized it all, returning the blood to her system. Her skin stopped itching. The burn in her muscles rescinded to a dull pain. Lilith scanned the room for her knife. She walked over, picked it up licking it clean, put it back in the sheath on her back.

I've missed some. Lilith hadn't found all the blood, yet. In the kitchen, she discovered paper towels stained blue. She devoured them. The paper caught on her tongue as she swallowed it down. Pulling off her boots and socks, she inspected them for blood.

A heavy sigh of relief escaped her lips. *At least I don't have to eat my boots.*

She dropped the boots next to the door. A mirror showed her exposed stomach. *A shirt would come in handy. No need to scare the locals.* She picked a shirt off the floor and gagged. *This shirt reeks! Like fairies, rolled in dragon feces.* She took another whiff the body odor, which smelled of chili powder as well. Still she draped the large shirt over her frame. *He needs to balance out his diet. If I didn't know better, I'd swear I could smell angel on it. No one is part angel.*

She walked into the bathroom and found the blue shirt with a long dark stripe of navy. Lilith blustered her lips. "Cotton has never been my favorite meal."

She scratched at the hair matted on her neck. She considered the shower, but figured cutting it all off would be easier. In the kitchen, she opened drawers, no scissors, and no sign of John.

"Screw it, I'll use a blade." She pulled her knife and grabbed a handful of hair.

A key rattled in the lock. Lilith could smell John on the other side, with bacon. He walked in, and took a step back at the sight of her.

"What?" Lilith asked cutting a chunk of matted ashen hair off her head. In moments the hair grew back out to its original length. She repeated the process for the rest of her hair, then scooped it up off the ground, and proceeded to choke it down. She coughed as the strands tickled her throat, pulling on a piece that caught on her back molar.

John held up a white waxed bag. "Do you eat people food?"

Lilith stalked across the room, leaned in, and smiled, grabbing the bag. "Amongst other things." Her stomach rumbled in protest again. She grabbed a greasy breakfast sandwich, took a seat on the bed, and scarfed it down. Salt and fat quivered on her tongue and slid down her throat.

She smacked her fingers to dust off the cornmeal. Still hungry. She considered eating John. But, the house reeked of lavender and vanilla. Someone else came over to the house, a lot.

Lilith checked again, John had blue eyes a sign of dragon blood. She smiled as he scratched his elbow. A patch of scaly dry skin. Probably related to one of her nephews. Original dragon lineage, even better. She pulled another sandwich out of the bag and made it disappear.

"Hey, one of those was for me." John crossed his arms over his chest.

"If you like I could eat you instead." Lilith licked her fingers and locked eyes with him.

John shook his head, as if he couldn't quite figure out what she meant, or didn't want to believe it.

"Mind if I raid your kitchen instead?" Lilith asked.

John slowly nodded his consent.

She opened a slim white paneled cabinet recoiling at the garlic she found inside.

"Ugh, gross." She pushed it out of the way. "Ah! Redemption." Lilith snagged a can of tuna from the pantry. She opened another cupboard to discover rice. "That'll do," she said. She got to work making up the rice and fish. *What am I going to do with him?*

"Could you maybe, put the knife away?" John asked from over by the door.

Lilith shrugged, tucking the knife out of sight. She rummaged in drawers, searching for a can opener. Kitchen cutlery rattled as she dug deeper. Thrilled at the array of knives she found, she grabbed one, and stabbed the can, working her way around the rim.

"I didn't mean pull out another one," John leaned on his door.

She laughed, and proceeded to rinse the blade off in the kitchen sink.

Dumping the tuna into a frying pan, left on the stove, she turned on the burner. After warming up the cold fish, she dumped the tuna in the pot of rice. Grabbing a spoon, she climbed up on the counter, where she sat crossed-legged, and dug into her meal.

"Right," John asked, "after your third meal, I'm sure you'll want to go find Zech. Can I give you a ride somewhere?"

"Who?" Lilith paused, looking away from the half-empty bowl.

"You muttered that last night. It was the only thing I could make out," John said.

"No. I need to get home." Lilith scratched her cheek. Maybe a shower wouldn't be such a bad idea.

"Where's that?" John asked.

"Don't know. Need to find it," Lilith said, her mouth full.

"You mentioned that hodags set up nests. Do we need to worry about that?"

Lilith looked up, rice dribbling down her chin, like a tiger interrupted mid-meal. "Probably."

John frowned. "Can you help me do something about that?"

"Is that what you want?" Lilith asked.

"Uh, yes."

Lilith smiled. "Done."

"What are you, anyway?" John asked. He moved towards his computer chair and tentatively sat down.

"Lilith." She finished the remaining tuna. She leaned over and put the pot in the sink. Swinging her legs down, headed for the pantry again. "And I need more food." She came out with a box of saltines in hand.

John picked up an empty bowl from the floor. He turned it over. "Lilith? Like mother of all monsters?" he asked.

"That's one way of looking at it. Surprised, you've heard that one."

"There are a couple of different versions." John's eyes darted around the room.

"I upset a Rabbi." She opened the crackers, shoving them in her mouth. Bits flew from her mouth as she continued to speak, "He got a little creative with my origin story."

John walked over to the sink and put the bowl in. "Right. What happened to all the blue blood?"

"I consumed it," Lilith said. She continued to munch on crackers. She finished two of the three sleeves in the box.

"Why would you do that?" John asked. "The iron content alone will make you sick." He turned to face her.

Iron content? He should be freaking out. What's with this kid? She thought, scrunching up her face. "Come on," Lilith said. "I'm not human." Lilith threw the empty wrapper in the garbage can by the counter. "Well, not anymore." Lilith looked at the empty box in her hand, and put it down on the counter. She headed back to the pantry and feigned at rummaging for food. She kept John in her sights.

"Then what are you?" John asked.

"Add it up," Lilith said. "If you're a creature fan, it won't be that hard. Self-healing and consumes blood."

John paced between the counter and the sink.

Lilith watched him, amused at how he puzzled out the options.

"You're not a vampire."

"I'm not?" Lilith asked. She walked out of the pantry.

John pointed at the window. "Light." Then to the mirror behind her. "Reflection. And I know I have garlic in the pantry. Plus I haven't been drained dry."

"Expert on vampires are we?" Lilith asked.

John shrugged. "You're right, I do like creatures."

"The consuming blood thing is exaggerated." Lilith headed for the fridge.

John gaped at her.

"It was the dark ages. You had to be there." She surveyed what the fridge had to offer. Styrofoam cups and take out boxes lined the top shelf. A bag of unopened spinach wilted in the crisper drawer.

"What do you eat?" John asked. He rubbed his throat and gulped. "Besides saltines?"

"Food," she said. She looked up from the fridge and smirked. "A lot of it. Also I get a little, eh, iffy if I lose blood and don't get it back." Lilith pointed at her head, turning her wrist as she spoke trying to indicate crazy. "Takes a while for my body to regenerate that. I'm lucky, the hodags didn't break skin in the orchard. Otherwise, I'd have to go hunting."

"How long does it take for your blood to replenish?" John moved in his computer chair as if looking for a strategic retreat.

"Years," Lilith said. She sighed, closing the fridge and opening the freezer.

John took a moment. "What about garlic?" John asked glancing at the pantry. "Does it chase you off?"

"No," Lilith scoffed closing the freezer door. "It's a root. I'm not keen on it."

"But, seriously you have a reflection." John said, pointing at the mirror.

"I made that one up to get out of Rome. True story. Ah, Romans. Good times." She laughed, pulling out a bag of frozen corn. "Most of what you hear about vampires is rumors, gossip, or stories that have twisted over the years."

"Crosses?" John pulled two pencils off his desk, holding them in a cross toward her.

"I have issues with the man upstairs. He's not my biggest fan, and I'm not fond of him. Crosses themselves won't do much to me." She ripped open the bag pulling out a handful of frozen kernels and shoving them in to her mouth.

"Oh." John dropped the pencils.

"If any of that worked on me, do you think I'd tell you?" Lilith munched on another handful of corn.

John gulped.

Lilith smiled. *I love it when they get scared.*

John sunk down into his computer chair. "Do you have family?"

Lilith put the empty bag of corn down on the counter. She took a breath. "No." She went over to the fridge and pulled out a stick of butter. "I'm it. Not for a lack of trying, of course." She leaned on the counter munching on butter. The fats slid around her mouth, she relished the taste.

"Go on."

"I wanted some company. Gets a little old when all your friends are dead. I tried a couple of things to see if I could make someone like me." Lilith licked the butter wrapper. Then held up a finger. "There were a couple of groups that tried to force me to make more vampires. Didn't go well." She waved her hand in the air, the wrapper flapping like a flag. "Myths and rumors about vampires also come from their failed attempts." She tore the wrapper up, chewed it up, and swallowed it down.

John cringed, and then scratched at his neck. "How did you become a vampire then?"

"Got hungry. Ate some fruit. Side effect of said fruit, you live forever." She sighed and continued using the counter as her podium. "I'm not so keen on apples."

"How old are you?" John asked.

"John," She said raising a hand to her chest in mock incredulity. "Things you shouldn't ask a lady."

John's head jerked back, grimacing. "Sorry, I mean, you don't sound, ancient."

"And, I'm no lady." Lilith raised her brows. "I excel at blending in. The language I learned to speak as a kid is long dead, but it was the first language ever. Every other language broke off of that. Gives me a bit of an advantage."

"Right, so not really offended about the age thing?" John asked.

"No. Why?" Lilith asked.

"I'm not sure you'll let me live." John bit his lip.

"I won't kill you." Lilith moved from the kitchen and sat down on the bed. "Others might, but I won't."

"Others?" John fiddled with the computer mouse on the desk.

"Couple of cults, and maybe a government or two." Lilith said. She got back up and went back into the kitchen raiding the cupboards for more food. "I have trouble keeping track of who is still in power over the years."

"Woah, I hadn't thought of that." John said.

"Yep," Lilith said. "Is the cross examination over?" She opened another cupboard and frowned. "Man, you need to go shopping."

"One last question, what happens when you die?" John asked.

"Depends on the death," Lilith said. "You saw what happened last night with that gash up my side?"

"You died last night?" John asked, bolting up right in his chair.

"Nope, but close," Lilith said. "Simple death, simple fix." She lifted the shirt exposing the fresh scar. "I'll feel this for weeks and have the scars until I die. When I die I go back to square one. Exactly the same as the day I turned. However, it hurts." Lilith could feel her joints throbbing.

John said, "What do you do about the pain?"

"Eat. You ask a lot of questions."

John swung back and forth in his chair. "Nervous habit. I still don't trust that you're going to let me live. You don't age?"

Lilith grabbed the knife from the sink.

John pushed himself away from Lilith, the chair's wheels squeaking. "Woah! What are you doing?"

"Do I need to show you what happens when I cut my hair again?"

John cocked his head. "I saw but if your hair can do that I don't understand why you scar."

"My body wants to keep me living. Scars are the quickest way to make that happen." Lilith jumped back up on the counter. "If I'm not careful, I can set bones incorrectly." She propped her left leg up on the counter and checked that it mended right. She ran her hands over the top of the dirty denim. "Then again, it can be fun to do that. I can show you."

John waved his hands in front of himself. "No! I'm good. Why would you even do that?"

"You've never wanted to change how you look? Or be able to disappear?"

"Not till last night." John picked up a silver key off his desk, turning it over in his hand.

"This has nothing to do with mythical creatures does it?" Lilith sighed, he was no fun.

"My girlfriend came in last night. Found me in a towel and you passed out on the bed."

"Bwahaha! Oh man, sucks to be you." Lilith held her side, the thought of some girl walking in on her covered in blue gore. "She must've thought you were into something real strange."

"Broke up with me right then. She thought you were covered in edible body paint." John frowned. "She said it tasted like berries."

Crap. Lilith frowned. "How much did she eat?"

"A little bit." John put the key down.

Lilith gulped.

"Will it hurt her?" John wrung his hands.

"The blood? No." Lilith jumped off the counter and gave him what she hoped was a reassuring smile. *The fact that I'll have to cut her open and get it back, might.*

"You're not allowed to eat my girlfriend," John got up and paced by the door.

"You mean ex-girlfriend."

John leaned on the door frame. "Seriously. No eating people."

"It's cute that you think you can stop me," Lilith said.

"What she consumed was solid. Couldn't we get her to pass it or regurgitate it?" John asked.

"Probably." Lilith sighed. *People are difficult.*

"Oh, and you can explain to Sarah why you were naked on my bed. I might have a chance at fixing things up with her," John said.

"I'm not helping you stalk your ex," Lilith polished off the remaining take-out in John's fridge. The smell in the kitchen improved. She now eyed the overflowing garbage can. *I'm not that hungry.*

"We are not stalking her. You need the blood back and I need to make sure she doesn't get hurt." John settled back into his chair at the computer.

"There is a big difference between saving someone's life and stalking them," Lilith said. She paced, her boots on either side of the carpet and linoleum between him and the kitchen.

"You said you'd help me." John leaned in closer to his computer screen.

"With the hodag problem." Lilith joined him at the desk, "Facebook? I had a book made out of faces once. Wouldn't shut up."

John grimaced. "Gross. I don't even what to know the mechanics behind how that worked."

The web page on the computer screen displayed a picture of a blonde named Sarah. Lilith scratched at her chin, examining the image. *Kind of scrawny.* Lilith thought.

John kept tracing the cursor back and forth over her relationship status. Single.

"I don't see how following her around until we find the right moment to grab her, is not a dodgy thing. We should probably be a little more concerned about the hodags showing up here, returning to the plasma center, or hunting your ex down."

The cursor stopped, and John looked her in the eye. "Why would they do that?"

"They pick up a scent and hunt it down," Lilith said. "They don't stop till they eat it or the little brutes have been killed. Right now, your work, apartment, and girlfriend smell like me." The smell of old workouts drifted up from the shirt. "I need a new shirt. This one smells like it's been soaked in a mix of spoiled milk and a flank of steak abandoned in a dumpster."

"Right, shirt, supplies, and then to the plasma center," John said. "Are we going to need to find some sort of special shop for the hodag repellent?"

"No, Walmart will work." Lilith sniffed the air, now stale sweet chili powder came off the shirt. She followed her nose. The odor wafted in from the open window. "Something smells weird." She looked out, concerned flashed across her face, hands gripping the sill.

"Yes, I get it," John crossed his arms over his chest. "The shirt smells bad."

"No," Lilith said. She glared at him. "Weird."

"Weird?" Jon looked at the garbage in the kitchen and then over at his laundry basket. "What kind of weird?" Jon joined Lilith at the window.

"How long has this window been open?" Lilith asked.

"Since last night. You reek when you repair, like someone frying rotten meat," John said.

Lilith's skin prickled. The air became still. "Run."

A large muscle-bound male burst through the open window. The glass shattered, the roar of thunder filled the room, shards refracting the early morning light.

John clapped his hands over his ears.

Lilith slammed him into the wall, shielding him from the raining glass. She grimaced. They cut into her skin, setting it ablaze. She gasped as some lodged in her flesh. "Don't look, John!"

Lilith glanced over her shoulder at the broad-chested guy with a double chin who stood on the bed. In his tanned hands, a glowing coil of thick rope. *Great, the thunder brother.*

9

DEATH BECOMES HER

"Let's go." Lilith grabbed John by the arm keeping her body between him and the angel, shoving him toward the door.

Thunder cracked, a trick of the thick rope, and a roar filled the room. Lilith could feel her stomach quiver as the noise grew in the space. Another crack. Mattress fluff rained through the air and a spring bounced near Lilith's feet.

"My bed!"

"Of all the things to be worried about!" Lilith couldn't tell if she was yelling or not past the roaring of the thunder rope. She shoved John and out the door and down the stairs "Go! Go! Go!" She gulped trying to make her ears pop.

"What was that?" John huffed as they ran away from the building.

"Safety first. Questions later. Is there a church nearby?" Lilith asked. She hadn't had a chance to make a note of who had her missing blood. The last thing she wanted to deal with was being killed by an angel.

"We're in Utah!" The sidewalk wide enough for them to run side by side.

"Yes or no?" Lilith asked. She picked up speed, ignoring the despair building up in her chest.

"One on every block." John pointed across the street to a one-level red brick building edged in white with an impeccable lawn.

A loud crack of thunder peeled out behind them.

The two headed for sanctuary in the building with the white steeple that pointed at the heavens.

Lilith yanked on the door. It rattled in defiance. "Come on!"

Another roar rang out, making her shudder.

"What happens if he hits me?" John asked. He leaned back against the door. His hand trembled against the glass.

She continued trying to pull the door open.

"What happens?" John repeated.

"The rope will obliterate you with sound. Then your soul will vibrate until you fall out of existence."

The glass trembled as sound waves from the weapon shuddered through her.

John pulling her around the side of the building. He yanked the door open and fled inside.

"How did you do that?" Lilith asked. She took deep steady breaths, which should have steadied her, but didn't.

"Unlocked." John moved down the darkened hall. Pale blue carpet disappeared into the dark.

"Odd." The torrent of noise continued to build outside. Lilith shuddered. "We need somewhere without windows."

"Right." John pulled on a door to his left. The edge of the light hit a small staircase that rose up into darkness.

"You have some strange luck kid." Lilith darted up the four steps. She could see the white brick wall and dark velvety curtains pulled closed to hide a stage. Once in the corner, slumped down, knees to her chest. *Sanctuary.* She pulled her boots off.

"Lilith, are we safe here?" John walked into the dark. He stumbled against a chair.

Lilith smirked as it clattered in the dark.

"Worship is between you and the guy on high. Churches, holy ground, and the like are safe regardless of where you stand with the man upstairs."

"That wasn't an angel. Must be some sort of demon, right?" John asked. He found the wall and sat down next to her.

"Worse." Her voice came out small, like she'd shrunk with the race from that monster.

"What could be worse than a demon?"

"A demon will reason with you. An angel, deals in absolutes."

"And destruction, apparently." John rubbed his face and sighed. "Are you sure that was an angel and not something else?"

Thunder rolled over the top of the building. Lilith cringed. "They've been around longer than me and have killed me more than enough times to call themselves whatever the hell they like."

John gulped. "He can't get in, right?"

"Yeah. All we have to do is wait him out."

Something buzzed in the dark.

"What is that?" Lilith asked.

"My phone." John's face lit with the LED glow. He glanced askance at Lilith. "Weirdo." Then frowned at whatever message had appeared on the screen.

"I don't understand why everyone carries around little devices that make them frown all the time." She crossed her arms over her chest, but tried to sneak a peek at the screen.

"Yeah." John shoved his phone back in his pocket. "I don't understand how you could be cool with dying all the time." His legs sprawled out in front of him.

Lilith couldn't look John in the eye. "You get used to it." She flicked her hand as if dismissing the notion, and forcing a smile. "After a while, it all becomes a grand joke. The list of what hasn't killed me is shorter than the things that have."

John's brow furrowed, he rubbed his hands on his knees. "Did you choose that?"

"No. I tried to end my life a long time ago." The roaring thunder outside stopped, doubling the quiet on stage.

John's head tilted. "After you became immortal, right?"

Lilith dragged her fingers across the short-piled carpet. "No. I became immortal by trying to kill myself."

John cheeks twitched, and brow contorted. "Contradictory,

much? That doesn't make any sense." He ran his hand over his face and bit at his knuckle. "Why would you try to kill yourself?"

She pulled a breath in letting it roll back out past her lips. "I needed to stop—everything." Tears welled, betraying her attempt at being clinical on the manner. "My thoughts were too loud and I didn't have any way to shut them up."

John sat quiet, listening in the dark.

The words tumbled out of her now, taking on a will of their own. No one listened to her about this. No one asked. "I questioned, everything." Lilith pulled her knees to her chest. She pushed the memories back down where they belonged. *I'd destroy that record if I could find it.* Somewhere out there, a record had been made of her early years, likely by the angels.

"Yeah, but that doesn't explain death by angel."

"I needed to be nothing. Because if we all came from somewhere. Wouldn't we go somewhere, after? I needed something stronger. Memory, action, thought, all of it had to go. I couldn't leave any of me behind." Lilith shook her head.

"You are fascinating. Scary and dangerous for sure, but I'd never want to forget you. You don't get to decide who remembers you, Lilith." John scooted a little closer to her.

Lilith pulled a deep breath in and continued, "If there is a power that can create, you'd think it be capable of destruction."

"Wondered about that. How did trying to die make you immortal?"

"My parents used to reminisce about where they came from, Eden and that there was another tree guarded by a Cheribum. She tilted her head back, resting it against the wall and looking at the ceiling.

"A Cherry-what-now?" John asked.

"She's the big boss. Her job is to annihilate anything that got near the tree. Problem is, you can grab a snack while she's busy attending to other things," Lilith said. "But my parents either didn't quite understand how the tree worked, or they left out key information. Either way…"

John caught on. "You don't die."

"Oh no. You die. Over, and over again." Lilith hugged her knees tighter to her chest, the unwanted memories of so many deaths washing over her till it felt like she drowned.

John pulled his knees up too, mirroring her pose. "Ouch."

"And, you don't age," Lilith hit her head on the brick wall behind her with a thud.

John shifted next to her. "In other words, the exact opposite of what you wanted."

Lilith nodded. Thoughts and feelings rumbled in her. When she shifted, the glass in her neck burned.

"Why the vendetta from on high?" John asked. "If I were them, I'd have tried to recruit you."

"Ask the almighty, he stopped talking to me," Lilith said. She rubbed her hands over her face. "My best guess, everyone is supposed to die."

1 0

JACKALOPES AND MERMAIDS

John tried not to think about the girl sitting next to him in the dark. Lilith may be ancient but just now she felt like a teenager. She brought to mind moments of darkness in his own life. Of course, he didn't want to think about those, but trying not to think about it, meant his thoughts headed that direction. That shared agony, made both of them painfully human. It tied them together.

John, however, grew up while Lilith still seemed like a kid. She'd never had to grow up, or maybe she couldn't, or deal with consequences. Something niggled at the back of his mind, he should be terrified of her, and everything he'd seen. All his experiences weaved back to Lilith. A gordian knot made out of all the information he read about as a kid.

His pocket buzzed, again.

He sighed, probably another message from Lisa. He'd have to handle that. Lisa, cute, but in a crazy cut-out-your-eyes kind of way, and viciously loyal. She wanted to know about the naked woman Sarah had seen covered in blue paint on his bed.

None of her business anyway. The only one he had to explain anything to was Sarah. If she'd listen.

Lilith sniffled, he smiled and put his arm around her. Lisa could wait.

John realized Lilith's world opened a whole new realm of possibilities. "Hold on, are dragons a thing?"

Lilith sniffled and blew her nose on the muddy brown t-shirt sleeve. "Yes. Hard to come by. But, yeah."

"Fairies?"

"Mermaids?"

"Jackalopes?" John threw the last one in as a joke.

Lilith nodded. "I've dealt with them all."

"Come on. Jackalopes? The invention of roadside taxidermists?"

"Sure and hodags were invented by a lumberjack." Lilith rubbed the palms of her hands into her eyes.

"Jackalopes are tourist souvenirs. Pieced together from roadkill," John said, but part of him knew that wasn't the case. If he stuck around Lilith, he might see more than just hodags and angels.

Lilith laughed. "If only. Do you know what happens when a Jackalope dies? It doesn't melt like a Hodag. Oh, no, it explodes and rains fiery death on everything around it. Great fire starter." She smirked. "Time to go." Lilith stood up, pulled the shirt up to her face and rubbed the remnants of her feelings off her cheeks.

"It's only been quiet for like a minute." John fidgeted in his spot. Bits and pieces from the past twenty four hours started to fall into place. "Wait, how does Iris know you?"

Lilith pursed her lips. "I'm her landlord. She lives at my house."

"Uh-huh. What is she?" John asked, drumming his fingers on the floor.

She crossed her arms, the irritation back, covering her pain. "Human."

"Right, and I'm part Jackalope."

"You want to know about Iris ask or her clan, ask me."

"I am asking. But I think I'll get more information out of Iris than you at this rate."

Lilith bit her lip. "There are certain creatures where curiosity will only bring you bushels of trouble."

"Really?" John raised a brow. "More than what I'm dealing with already?" He stood.

"You got a point. She used to be Queen of the fairies," Lilith said.

"She was crazy?" John asked.

"No, like she set up a contract with me to protect her clan from the angels. She broke the contract, and the consequence is, she became human." Lilith walked back down the stairs and into the hallway with John by her side.

"Nice of you to let her live at your house," John said. The hallway lead back to a quiet foyer.

"Yeah. Also easier to keep an eye on her. He's gone, I think. Why don't you head on out there?" Lilith stared at the sunshine pouring through the glass doors. She seemed to be assessing her options.

"What?" John jumped away from the door like it was venomous.

"Walk out there," Lilith said again. Hands on hips and pursing her lips.

"No way." John moved even further away from the door. "Not with that thing out there."

"You'll be fine," Lilith said waving a hand, dismissing the concern. "He's probably gone by now."

"Probably?" John asked. "I don't want to risk my life on probably."

"Those hodags could be snacking on your ex as we speak," Lilith said. "The sooner we can critter proof your apartment, work, and ex. The better things will be."

"Alright," John shifted his weight between his feet. He crept out of the first set of double doors and scanned the skies. Glancing back, Lilith motioned him on.

John stood in the empty parking lot looking up. No thunder. No burly dude with a rope. He heard the click of the chapel door behind him and Lilith came to join him.

"Nothing," John said searching the skies. "Where did it go?"

"Good," Lilith headed in the direction of the center. "Off we go."

John watched the skyline. Storm clouds hung over the mountain range ahead like a veil, the falling snow on the range looked like antique lace.

A leaf skittering behind him caused him to pick up speed. A dark blue stain soaked the neckline of the shirt. "Woah, look at the back of your shirt!"

"Yeah," Lilith turned the corner, John's apartment in sight. "Blood from the attack. I'm going to need some help later."

"With what?" John asked. The houses on the road they passed, were all modern construction. An occasional old farmhouse broke the line, but they wouldn't last long as progress continued in the valley.

"Removing the glass from my neck," she said as they closed in on John's apartment building. She touched them with light fingers. "It hurts something fierce."

"I hate to tell you this, but that is going to hurt more," John moved towards a dark blue car.

"Yep."

"Are you going to have to eat that shirt?" John asked unlocking the car door letting them into the vehicle.

"Yep." She slid into the car. A variety of fast food wrappers made a patchwork pattern throughout the interior of the car, a quilt of bright colors and grinning mascots. John pushed the trash off the seat and onto the floor. A crunch came from beneath Lilith's boot as she sat down.

"That sucks," John said buckling his seatbelt. "I like that shirt." Looking up at his apartment he asked, "Do you think my apartment will be safe anytime soon?"

"Go up now, if you like," Lilith said shifting in her seat. "They don't tend to hang around." She leaned her arm on the door as John started the car. "They show up, they disappear. The limited experience I do have normally involves me dying."

"Is there any other way you attract them?" John asked the traffic light ahead as it turned red.

"Let's see," Lilith rubbed her chin. "Someone uses God's name to curse me," she held up a thumb and continued, "When I heal large wounds," the pointer finger followed. Extending her middle finger she said, "And when I come back from the dead. Seems to be about it. I'm not doing anything new."

"Huh," John said. "I wonder why?"

"Damned if I know," she said as John parked the car. "Wait, why did we drive here? This is walking distance from your house." Lilith got out of the car. "I can see the plasma center from the parking lot."

"I don't know," John said. "Habit?"

Lilith shook her head and walked towards the Walmart. A patch of grass ran down the middle of the parking lanes and here and there people stood or talked. John jumped as a box next to Lilith's leg erupted with barking. He looked in to see mutts with big eyes.

When Lilith backed away, an array of fluffy brown and white spots began wrestling and playing again. Lilith joined him next to the box and the puppies stopped playing instead growling, howling, and snarling.

A tan man sat on the bench in plaid and denim watching them.

"How much?" she asked.

"Free, but I don't think they like you," he replied, coming over as if guarding the pups.

"I think you're right." Lilith took a couple of steps back. "Have a good one," she headed to the front entrance of the store.

The puppies went back to playing. John watched Lilith who stood in front of the automatic sliding door with a frown on her face. John walked up beside her. It to slid open without a problem.

"Thinking of getting a pet?" John asked as they headed for the carts.

"Maybe not from that lot. A little scraggly for my taste."

"Why didn't the door open for you?" John asked grabbing a cart.

"They don't work for me," Lilith glared back at the door. "It's like they don't recognize I'm there."

The store stretched out before them, a warehouse stuffed with a variety of products and consumables. Empty except for an occasional employee with an empty pallet jack passing between the aisles.

"What time is it?" Lilith walked down the main hall, the cart squeaking beside her.

Pulling out his phone and his face crinkled up like a discarded tissue, John replied, "early."

"Is that a bad thing?" She passed a display of red and green. On one shelf jolly Santas waved. The merchandise descended on the unsuspecting consumer although it was early November.

"No," he glanced over at the holiday section. "You think they'd give it a break till December. I guess they could smash all the holidays together."

"Uh huh," Lilith moved away from the section, turning down the baking aisle. She stopped at the vinegar and grabbed everything available on the shelf, the liquid sloshing as she put the jugs in the cart.

"That's a lot of vinegar," John said leaning over and looking at the empty shelf.

"This is the main ingredient of hodag repellent," Lilith held up one of the bottles, giving it a shake, the liquid swirling and forming a tiny funnel in the top of the bottle. "They can't stand the smell, drives them crazy."

"That wasn't crazy last night?" John followed her down the aisle.

"It'll drive them crazy like hiding from an ex you don't want to see," Lilith ran her hand along spices on the shelf, "last night was more of a frenzy."

"Could you train them?" John halted as Lilith stopped.

"What, like a pet?" Lilith shook her head in response."No."

"Just a thought," John pushed the weighted cart down towards the end of the aisle. The cart clicking as it rolled over the floor. She grabbed all the sage, rosemary and thyme off the shelf.

"What no parsley?" John asked.

Lilith ignored him, continuing to the cloves and grabbing the remaining bottles.

"Is this the biggest thing of salt they have?" Lilith asked looking over the shelf at the one-pound cylinders.

"Looks like it," John said.

Behind them another cart squeaked. John looked back and a guy in blue jeans and a blue and white striped t-shirt gave him a crooked smile.

Weird. John kept following Lilith.

"How'd you come up with this recipe anyway?" John asked. Plus size shirts and skirts announced their arrival in apparel.

"Well, the plague was a big help," Lilith grimaced at some neon shorts. "There was some trial and error, but this recipe kept the pests at bay so we could get near plague victims."

"Why would you be going anywhere near plague victims?" The cart knocked a row of hanging navy shirts proclaiming, "Go Cougars!" in bold white print. On the other side of the rack bright red shirts toting the phrase "Go Utes!" fought for space. The annual holy war between the two local football teams must be nearing.

"The corpses had things I wanted," Lilith moved through the jungle of clothing. She grabbed a bra and threw it in the cart. "It's hard to loot corpses if your crew keeps getting sick and dying."

"You came up with a way to prevent catching the plague so you could loot?" John asked.

"Yep," Lilith headed towards a table of cotton shirts. "And when we got caught, I traded the recipe to keep us from hanging."

"You can't die," John pushed the cart between ugly Christmas sweaters and hoodies lined with soft fleece. "Why would you do that?"

"They were a good crew." Lilith grabbed a maroon shirt and threw it in the cart. She moved out of the clothing section, headed for the door.

"Where are you going?" John asked looking behind him at the row of registers. "Checkout is back that way."

"Leaving," Lilith walked past the in-store nail salon. "I'm hungry."

"Aren't you forgetting something." John waved his hand over the shopping cart.

"What?" Lilith looking at her selections. "None of this is tagged. It won't set off an alarm."

"We haven't paid for this," John pulled the cart back.

Lilith grabbed the front of it. "I'm not going to pay for it," she tugged the cart towards her. She sidled up next to John, nudging him forward. "Come on, let's go." She pushed the cart forward and out the double doors.

"Excuse me," the guy from earlier with the striped t-shirt said, "Are you planning on paying for that?"

"No," Lilith replied, a childlike smile on her lips.

"Right, then. I'm Officer Michaels." He flashed a badge, though he wasn't wearing a uniform. "Come with me."

"We should have paid," John said. "What were you thinking?" He turned to continue reprimanding Lilith, who was gone along with the t-shirt and bra.

The officer placed his hand on John's shoulder. "Come on, John, let's have a chat." He opened a door to a backroom of the store. It looked like security. John had trouble placing the cop's accent sounded Australian, but not.

"Who's your mate?" the police officer asked.

"Not much of a friend. She took off," John said. He folded his arm across his chest. "Doubt I'll see her again."

The officer indicated he should have a seat. John sat down on the other side of the gray table.

"Then what was the nature of the relationship?" the officer sat up straight, leaning forward. "Have you known her very long?"

"I met her yesterday," John shifted in his chair. "Don't know much about her to be honest." John looked around large monitors displaying video feed from around the store. *Probably best not to mention the hodags, the immortality thing, or those damn scary angels.*

"Can you give me an account of your time together?" The officer squinted at John with dark amber eyes.

"Yeah, she showed up at my work," John winced as he tried not to think about the gory events at the plasma center. "Then we crashed at my apartment for the night." *Boy did things get weird there.* "Then we went to the store."

"I see," the officer said. His strong square jaw clenched as he stared John straight in the eyes. "Have you slept with her?"

"No!" John's face twisting like he had sucked on a lemon. *Dear God, no.* Shaking his head. "What does that have to do with a cart full of spices and herbs anyway?"

"Good. Glad to hear it." The officer turned a page over in the folder, not answering his question. "Sleeping with her would be a bad idea."

"No kidding," John said. "I think you'd have to be half-mad to consider it."

Officer Michaels laughed. He ran his hand through gentle dark curls. "Now for some good news. The store won't be pressing charges."

John asked, "Really?"

"Yup," the officer said. "I'm sure there are things you need to be taking care of, eh?"

"Uh, yeah." John thought of the hodags and having no clue of how to make the mix. He could at least pay for the cart of groceries and try himself. John smiled. The guy across from him looked like an angel sent from heaven.

"These things happen. But I'd be careful of the company you keep," The officer got up and opened the dark blue door.

"I guess so," John took a deep breath. "Am I free to go?"

"Sure are," the officer flashed a smile. "See you around, John."

11

BACK TO THE GRINDSTONE

Zech sighed. John smelled a bit like Lil, decay and cinnamon. He bit the inside of his cheek to help with pressing down the memories of time they spent together. The boy also smelled of copper and lemon, but that could be explained easy enough by his job with Iris. The one odor that puzzled Zech was the undertone of sulfur mixed with spoiled summer apples, he hadn't caught a whiff that strong since the legion hunted down the last son of Cain.

He walked out of the store security office wondering if John could be related. When a meaty hand grabbed him by the collar.

"You. Training now," Gabe said.

Zech shook him off. "We got a skull to track down." He walked out the store's automatic doors and took a deep breath of the chilled air.

"We also need to maintain our daily rituals," Gabe said. "Remember how you took off and left me to clean up the mess at the bleeding center?"

"Yes," Zech said. "You brought the hodags west. I figured, you should clean up after them."

"I didn't bring them past the river, they were already here," Gabe said. "Also, you are not supposed to leave my side." Gabe fell in to step next to Zech, feet thudding on the asphalt as they crossed the parking lot.

Zech paused. "You didn't bring the hodags?"

"No, but it didn't take much for them to lead us to the abomination." Gabe wrapped one hand over the other cracking his knuckles. "The last time you disappeared, Cheri had a word with me."

"I'm sure you had more than a few words for her. Did you list all my sins or spend all your time praising her?" Zech asked.

Gabe clapped his hand on Zech's shoulder. "Blasphemy doesn't suit you," he said. "If we don't deliver the skull. She says she'll intervene, and you'll be moving on."

"Like to Australia?" Zech raised his brows.

"To a place where you'll never be able to vex me again," Gabe seemed pleased at the idea of Zech's execution.

"You'd miss me." Zech laughed. "Not quite ready to move on to the next plane. Guess we better find that skull. I still don't think it'll work."

Gabe shook his head. "The older the skull, the stronger the link between the realms."

"Yeah, but who wants to talk to Cain?" Zech asked. "Everything I've heard about the guy makes him sound like a real jerk."

"Then you two will get along," Gabe stretched his shoulder causing it to pop. "I think you're more concerned about what will happen to the abomination when we get hold of the skull. I wouldn't be to worried, dying a few more times won't be the end of her."

Zech grimaced, he knew that Lil felt every death long after she came back.

"The abomination will serve her purpose," Gabe crossed his arms over his broad chest. They had reached the edge of the parking lot and stood on the sidewalk as cars zoomed past them on the main road.

"Lilith. Her name is Lilith," Zech said. The palm of his left hand crackled. He considered pulling the blade from his hand and teaching Gabe a lesson.

"You need to be careful with the battles you choose." Gabe approached the crosswalk and pushed the button. It chirped in response.

Zech leaned against the cold metal of the pole. "I'd fight the whole legion for her."

"Cheri warned me you may get difficult." The red hand changed to a white walking figure. The two crossed the road together. "Let's train and clear our heads."

"Couldn't we count the hodags from last night?" Zech asked.

Gabe placed a meaty hand to his chin, rubbing his fingers along his jawline. "No."

Ahead a white shack with red trim sat bleakly alone near the road. The Shiver Shave Shack closed for the season just beyond it. On one of the abandoned picnic tables, a thin girl in a bright blue fuzzy hoodie sat swinging her feet, black boots unable to touch the gray gravel. In front of her, a huge box of donuts. The child wolfed a donut down, glaze sticking to cherub cheeks. Long wild brown hair with hints of red and gold fluttered in a passing breeze. Deep brown eyes fixated on Zech and Gabe as they approached.

"Is one of those for me, little one?" Zech asked.

The girl scowled and began to eat another donut from the box, crumbs falling on sky blue fleece pants. She licked her fingers as she finished, and pulled a cream filled donut from the box.

Gabe gulped. "We have work to do."

"I thought you wanted to train?" Zech asked, glancing over at Gabe.

"Mission first," Gabe said.

The little girl hummed to herself as Gabe and Zech walked past the shave ice shack which sat not far beyond doughnut-girl.

Zech could feel the girl watching him as they left. A chill ran across his shoulders. He shuddered. "Right. I think the abomination has a stash nearby. One I didn't know about. Might be worth checking out."

"Can you find it?" Gabe asked. He perked up like a bulldog presented with a favorite toy.

"I have a couple of leads," Zech said. Heading down the road toward the address Iris had given him. "But there may be a fairy involved."

Gabe spit on the ground. "Quick and tiny fiends of damnation."

"If there is a clan you can murder the lot of them," Zech said.

Gabe held a grudge against all fae-kin after an encounter with one clan that left him naked on an ice float.

He then added, "After I talk to them."

Gabe smashed and squished imaginary fairies with his hands.

"Gabe? Maybe it'd be best if I checked this lead out myself," Zech said. Iris smelled like a fairy, for all he knew the old woman may just be really keen on lemons and pennies. Adding Gabe to the situation did not seem wise. He had to think of something to distract the big lug. "Have we done a sweep since we got to this part of the country?" Zech asked.

"No," Gabe said. "We've been too busy dealing with the abomi-nations messes." Gabe tilted his head a loud crack came from his neck.

"Right then," Zech said. "Why don't you do a sweep. I'll see whether this is one of the abomination's stashes. Divide and conquer."

"You're just trying to get rid of me." Gabe crossed his arms over his chest.

True. The pair where now within a couple houses of the address. "No, I'm trying to fulfill the mission of the Legion. But really, would you rather be sitting around talking with some old lady or out on a hunt?"

Gabe scratched at his round chin. "You may be on to something."

"Can't be too careful," Zech said. "Especially when we had a pack of hodags running wild. Are we sure we got them all?"

"You may be onto something," Gabe repeated, then smiled and stretched his arms behind him cracking his other shoulder. "You scout out the stash. I'll do a sweep of the area."

"Are you sure?" Zech asked. "I can come with you be an extra set of eyes?" Zech glanced askance at Gabe. He knew questioning his abilities would make him all the more eager to take off.

"I've got this," Gabe took off, thunder followed him.

Zech chuckled and held up his arm as a blast of wind hit his face from Gabe's departure. If he could get hold of the skull, it would get Cheri off his back for a while. Then he'd be free to muck about for a bit, maybe even spend some time with Lil. Probably not the best plan, but then again he wasn't exactly known for wise decisions.

12

THREE'S A CROWD

There's my hardened criminal!" Lilith waved and cracked a smile, as John came out of the store. "What took you so long?"

John kept walking past Lilith shaking his head, his breath tumbling out of his mouth and nostrils and in the chill air, curling up like smoke. He headed to his car, keys jangling and unlocked the door before getting in.

She caught up to him and tried to open the passenger door, still locked. *He's mad?* She knocked on the window. "Where are you going?"

John rolled down the passenger window a crack. "Away from you."

Lilith didn't like that answer.

John kept his eyes forward. "You're trouble. Why are you even still here?"

"I was coming to get you out," Lilith stretched up, reaching up for the sky. Now wearing the maroon shirt, her bare arms capped with black gloves. The serpent tattoos looked like they were ready to chase the clouds away. "Did you think I'd leave you in there?"

"Yes," John got out of the car and slammed the door shut.

People whizzed past fast food joints lining the street. Bright colorful signs tried to lure people in from their morning commute.

"I had a plan and everything!" Lilith walked around to the other side of the car, leaning on the closed door. She crossed her arms, shuddering as she turned to face him.

"No, you didn't." John shook his head the tightness of his mouth revealing how hard he was trying not to smile.

"Yeah, you're right. I didn't have a plan." Lilith smiled and then laughed. "But, all the supplies for the hodag spray are on your back seat."

John looked in the back of his car. Looked at Lilith and back in the car. He turned around and thudded his forehead on the roof and wrapped his arms around his head. His shoulders began to shake.

"Are you crying?" Lilith asked. Or could he be laughing? Lilith had fallen out of the habit of being considerate, let alone aware of others feelings. *Why do I even care?* But she did.

John turned around gripping his side and started laughing out loud. "You used my interrogation to steal the stuff and then broke into my car."

She moved away from the chilled metal of the vehicle. "I was going to get you out. I mean someone has to cut the glass out of the back of my neck."

John shook his head and wrapped his arm around her shoulder like a big brother. "Let's go take care of that." He smiled and chuckled as he let go of her to open the door.

Lilith frowned, it felt nice to be warm. "To the plasma center!" She declared punching the air as she walked to the other side of the car.

John looked over at Lilith as she got in. "You ate my shirt didn't you?"

"Yep," her nose scrunched up. "It was awful." Her neck burned, hands curled up into fists. "I'll need you to cut the glass out of my neck. Soon."

John started the car. "I liked that shirt."

"I'll get you a new one. Not covered in my blood." Lilith burped.

John laughed as they drove across the street and parked outside the plasma center's employee entrance at the back of the building. "I can only imagine the disaster we are about to walk in and there are security tapes. What are we going to do about that?" John asked as he got out of the car.

Lilith shrugged. She opened the back door pulling out the supplies. "Delete the tapes. Clean up the mess."

John pulled out his keys as they walked up to the employee entrance. He opened the door, alarm beeping. He deactivated the alarm and they walked down the hall and into the building.

Lilith followed, frowning at what she couldn't find. No smells. That, and why was John being nice? He should have driven off and left her in the parking lot. Cut his losses. But he cared about the people around him, even her.

Lilith joined him in the front lobby.

"It's so clean," John said. He ran his hand over the desk, which had been toppled the night before. The front doors glinted in the sunlight.

Lilith walked over took a closer look. She sniffed the door frame. Nothing. It was as if the center had just opened. The bloody mosaic from the night before gone.

She shuddered. "That's weird." Her nostrils twitched, taking a deep breath as she turned around. No iron from the blood spilled, no bleach, the lack of anything niggled like a maggot in her brain. "I smell nothing," she said.

"What do you mean?" John asked.

She shook her head. "This building smells wrong. No sweat, no blood, no hodags, no cleaning chemicals, nothing." She darted to the donor bays in the back.

John ran to keep up. "We saw the hodags destroy this place."

Lilith's side itched, she scratched at the new scar. "I have the marks to prove it. I've never seen anything like it."

"I guess we should get going on mixing up the repellent," John walked back towards the front lobby.

"We won't need it." Lilith ran her hand over the mended wall. "Looks like we didn't need to knick that stuff after all."

John gave her a sharp look over his shoulder. "We?"

Lilith shrugged in response. She put the bags down on the counter, the plastic crinkling as they settled. The glass cut a little deeper in her neck, the pain flamed up into the base of her skull, she could hear her teeth grinding as she suppressed a yelp. Her eye twitched. "I can't take it anymore. Is there somewhere you could cut this glass out?"

"Not here. Employees will be showing up for the morning shift." John stood on the other side of the counter shoving his hands in his pockets, like a child trying to avoid doing the dishes.

"It'd be easier to think if I wasn't being repeatedly stabbed," she said.

"Didn't you say you lived around here?" John asked.

"I think I live around here," she said.

"You think? How do you not know where you live?" he asked.

Lilith rubbed her face and sighed. She didn't have words for this. "Everything changes," she clenched her hands to keep from thinking.

"Yeah," he said. He waited as if expecting an explanation.

"Think about the first place you can remember," she said.

"Ok, like home?" he asked.

Lilith cringed. She tried not to think of her own first memories of home. "Sure. But your first memory of it."

John laughed. "Oh man. Okay so this one time, my cousin dared me to jump off the roof using a plastic bag as a parachute and I think the only thing that kept me from splitting my head open was I landed in my mom's blackberry bushes."

"Are the blackberry bushes still there?" Lilith asked.

"No. We pulled them out when they started taking over the yard," he said.

"Alright, think about what else has changed."

"A lot," John said.

"When I first showed up in this part of Utah. It wasn't a state, no roads, no trails, and the best part, no people," she pulled out one of the jugs of apple cider vinegar and popped it open, taking a swig. She enjoyed the burn of the liquid as it went down her throat. She wiped her mouth with the back of her hand. "Anything I knew is gone. I belong here, but I don't."

"Sounds a bit like when I went back to my elementary school over the summer. The bricks were all still there, the hallways felt tiny. The hook I used to have to stretch up to hang my coat in kindergarten, I'd have to bend down to reach. The teacher I had retired. I felt out of place," John rubbed at his shoulder.

She put the lid back on the vinegar with a pop. "Yeah, so when I've been away for a bit, it can be disorientating until I learn the lay of the land again. I know I need to get back there, but I can't quite remember why."

John frowned. "That doesn't sound like a good thing. Let's find your house and we'll sort out the glass there. Deal?"

"We have other things to worry about first. That ex probably reeks of your scent which could bring the hodags to her door," Lilith said.

"Do they come out during the day?" John asked.

"I've only ever run into them at night. Then again I've never seen them west of the Mississippi before." Lilith scratched at her scalp. She tugged at the roots of her hair. "Creatures normally don't leave their home turf."

"I think getting you home takes priority," he said.

"She also has a bit of my blood in her gut," Lilith said.

"One thing at a time. The blood isn't going anywhere and if it does, then I won't have to worry about you gutting my girlfriend," John said.

"Ex-girlfriend," she said.

"Working on fixing that." John rubbed a hand over his face. He played with the handle of the bag on the counter.

"Hope springs eternal with you. I'd cut my losses." Lilith leaned against the counter behind her crossing her arms over her chest.

"Not ready to give up just yet. I have a list of problems to deal with." He put the apple cider back in the bag. It hit the counter with a thud. "You know with my place destroyed, I'm going to need somewhere to stay. If we find your place, I could crash there." He placed his hands on his hips, posing like a superhero.

"No."

"It'd be a day or two tops." John leaned forward on the counter giving her a big goofy grin.

"My house has issues." Lilith pursed her lips.

"Obnoxious roommates? Or plumbing type issues? I'm sure it has a front door. So it's doing better than my place."

Running her hand over her face, Lilith shifted her jaw back and forth causing it to click. *This is a terrible idea.* She stared at him, sizing him up. He'd handled hodags, regeneration, and angels well enough. If he couldn't keep up, she could always see about turning him to leather. "When we reach the house, do not touch anything. Do not speak to anything. Including the walls. Do not leave my sight," she said. At least she could try to keep him from getting himself killed.

"What?" John stood up straight as if at attention. "Why? It can't be that dangerous, Iris lives there."

"Iris is probably one of the more dangerous things on my property." She stretched her shoulder till it popped. "Wait, Iris works here."

"Yeah."

"Could you get her address?" she asked.

"Yeah," he said. "I mean, I probably shouldn't, but it is your house." John came around to the other side of the desk and turned on the computer. The keys clacking beneath his fingers as he looked up Iris's address. He looked up and smiled. "We know where you live."

"Let's go then," she said. Her neck burned and it'd be good to get back to the property. She heard the side door clank shut and caught a whiff of something intoxicating. Blood, her blood. "By the way your ex is here."

"How do you know?" John asked. He smoothed his hair and straightened his shirt.

"Heard the side door close. Smelled the blood," she said.

"She can't see me with you." He bit at his thumb.

Lilith rolled her eyes. "Why not?"

"Never mind. Hide." John tried to push Lilith down beneath the counter.

She slapped his hand away. "I'm not hiding."

A lean girl stalked into the room like a leopard on the prowl.

"That's not Sarah," Lilith said.

"This is so much worse," John said. "That's Lisa." He chewed on the edge of his lip.

Lisa stalked up towards them, hips swaying and heels clicking on the linoleum.

"Hello," Lilith said. She raised a brow. *Why does she smell like my blood?*

"Hi, John," Lisa said. Her amber eyes lingered over him. Lilith knew that look. Delilah made eyes like that at Samson. If John got entangled with her, he'd never get back together with his ex. *She's going to hate me.* Lilith thought throwing an arm around John's shoulder.

"John, who is this?" Lisa asked, hands on her hips.

"I'm a friend from out of town," Lilith pulled John in closer, squeezing his shoulder which tensed up at the attention from her fingers.

"Friend?" Lisa pulled on a black pendant that hung around her neck, fingernails clicking on the jewelery.

"Yes, you've heard of friends, right?" Lilith stared at the pendant. She knew it, somehow.

"From Minnesota?" Lisa tucked the dark carving back into her white collared shirt. She crossed her arms over her chest.

"We should get going." Lilith linked her arm through his and started pulling him away from Lisa, as if dragging prey away from another predator.

"Don't forget about later, John," Lisa called.

They had reached the exit.

"I promise, I'll explain." John called back as Lilith yanked him out of the building. She flung the dark brown door open and it hit the wall with a crack.

"Why? Why would you do that?" John shook her loose as he

threw his hands in the air. "I could have snuck you out of the building while Lisa was doing prep."

"Something's not right with her," Lilith said.

"No. There's something not right with you," John headed down the road behind the plasma center.

"There's something odd there." Lilith looked back at the building. "I can't put my finger on what."

John turned the corner heading down the sidewalk. "Lisa is not odd."

The idea nagged at Lilith. "Wait, you like her. Those mysterious eyes and raven locks entrance you." Lilith batted her eyelashes and cupped her hands under her chin.

"Quit it. It's not like that." He shot a glare her way. Leaves scuttled down the sidewalk behind them being pushed by the wind. Fences started appearing and modern homes hid behind them. Yards with swing sets and slides sat quiet.

"Yet." Lilith wiggled her thick eyebrows. "You could go for it. You are single after all. What are you two doing later, anyway?"

"None of your business," John sped ahead.

"Can I come?" She asked, scampering up beside him. "I make excellent dinner company."

"No. I've seen how you eat," he said.

Lilith's tongue tingled. That meant the wards on her house were still in place. She turned into a clean cut yard, dead grass crunching under her boots. She kept moving, branches littered the ground, crunching under foot.

John stumbled behind. "Why are we sneaking through a backyard?"

"Not sneaking. At my house, the front door is easier to get to through the backyard," Lilith walked up to a fence with old wooden posts and two lines of warped barbed wire. She slipped between them.

John followed, cussing as a piece of barb grabbed hold of his shirt ripping at the cotton. Like a hand trying to hold him from entering the property.

Lilith laughed as John stumbled through and kicked a small

pile of rocks that clattered and scattered across the fence line. Quartz, agates, and obsidian chunks glittered in the sun.

"Come on, keep up," Lilith said.

John scrambled to catch up. He passed through the line of blue spruces guarding the property line, needles and small pinecones under their feet. A large shed with flaking white paint also watched them as they crossed the backyard.

Lilith broke the silence. "This used to be the front of the house before the road went in." They walked up to the country rambler. Lilith headed towards the gate with white latticework and disappeared down a cement staircase. Bits of quartzs embedded into the walls reflected light like stars.

Lilith traced her fingers over the cement, catching at her skin. She looked back up at John, the sunlight framed him, leaving his features lost in the shadows.

"If you do anything stupid, I can't help you." Lilith watched him as he descended the staircase. "Remember the rules."

13

WHO'S THAT KNOCKING AT MY DOOR?

Iris suffered. She shifted her hips and tried to find a more comfortable position in her seat at the kitchen table. A sliding glass door overlooked the backyard. The blades of grass all lost their summer colors, instead of dark greens, yellows and browns peppered the ground.

Iris shivered and pulled her fuzzy pink robe closer around her. Grateful to be inside and warm. Even though she felt brittle, like a dead oak tree. Stiff when she walked, everything seemed to creak and groan. She'd out live any human, but for her kind, she only had a little time left. In her mind, she had one oath to keep. Free the clan. She would not wither away, her death would have meaning.

Skies of blue cracked through the gray clouds. She smiled, the vast stretch made her think of her first voyage across the seas. They flitted amongst flying fish, rode on the back of sea giants, even dined with merkind. The clan lived and thrived best when on the move. She could almost smell the sea, it called to her bones.

Her knee twinged, bringing her back to the present in the quiet kitchen. The only thing that ached worse than her feeble body was seeing the clan bound to one place. A whole world to explore and they were trapped in a basement. She clenched her jaw. Damn the angels for attacking and the Hag for taking advantage.

She leaned back in the wooden chair, it squeaked in protest. She organized her thoughts like a black widow preparing to spin its web. The contract bound in iron lay somewhere in the halls deep below the house. The clan were bound to protect the property, her word kept her from pursuing it herself. Blasted words, first used by man to bind her folk, but the clan learned to use them for their own. Fae everywhere gained power and strength when oaths and promises were kept.

A gentle tingle ran across her cheek. She looked up as The Hag strode across the yard, John tumbling through the fence after her.

Such a trusting lad, Iris thought. She scraped a finger along the edge of her empty breakfast plate. She watched the pair like a hawk tracking a field mouse. They disappeared down to the basement entrance of the house.

"Connor," she called. A rattle came from the air vent.

"Yes, Mum," Connor said.

"You have company," Iris picked up the morning dishes. The fork and knife clattered as she put them in the sink.

"Aye," Connor's voice came up from the vent in the floor. "The stones disturbed gave us a heads up that The Hag is here."

"Turns out the lad decided to pay us a visit as well. Would you look out for him while he's down there? See what The Hag wants with him." She grabbed a cup from next to the sink and turned on the tap. Water splashed in the bottom of the glass. She took a long draw. Not morning dew, but it would have to do.

"Nothing good," Connor said.

"Perhaps we can be a boon," Iris put the cup down, clinking against the marble countertop. She stared at the vent in the floor, trying to catch sight of her son. He knew better than to stand where he could be seen. Part of The Hag's new contract. She couldn't see any of her clan.

"And what? In return he'll get us the contract? Leave it be." Connor's voice echoed in the duct.

"He's one of us dear. I'm sure of it now and we look out for our own." She ran her hands over the gray braid that hung to her shoulder. Thick dark locks now dulled and thinned with age. It felt like brambles beneath her worn fingers, instead of like thick purple corn silk when she still retained her true form.

"Can't be more than a thimble's worth in him," Connor said.

"If a drop of our blood runs through his veins, we claim him. Or did you all start dividing and multiplying since I last saw you?" Iris asked. She took the chance to add the barb that there had been no new kin since they had been contracted to the house.

"You know that is not how it works." The words seemed to barely make it past the grate.

"A child or two before I die isn't too much to ask." She cinched her robe around her waist.

"You are fixated on nothing but impossible tasks," Connor said.

"You have an other. I don't see what the problem could be." She tapped a fuzzy slipper on the tiled floor.

"Last I checked that's between me, Agnes, and the sheets. No one else," Connor punched the vent.

Iris smiled, so easy to rile this one. When one of these moods hit, it was easy to direct him towards her goal. "So it is. But we look out for our own."

"That we do," Connor said. "The Hag is at the door. Got to go."

The hum of the fridge filled the kitchen. Iris smiled, the clan would befriend him, The Hag would play her part, such a selfish creature. John would see the right thing to do. He'd get the contract, and they'd roam again.

Iris went to get dressed. As she walked through her front room, she noticed someone walking up the black asphalt drive. Lisa, her hips swished and swayed like autumn leaves falling to the ground. Iris pushed down the jealousy at how fluid the young girl moved.

Best to scare her off . The last thing Iris needed was someone running John off, or worse, distracting him from what she needed to happen.

The girl didn't approach the front door. Instead, she prowled around to the side of the house and out of sight of the large window.

Iris tied her robe and threw the front door open. The white

screen door opened with a clang as she pushed her way out. "Lisa?" she called as she turned the corner, past a bare plot of earth, spring bulbs buried beneath. The smells of rich earth helped calm her.

"Iris?" Lisa asked. The two women faced each other as if preparing to duel, except with complements and niceties. "Where you looking for me, dear?" Iris asked.

Lisa gulped, her eyes darted to the side. "Yes, of course. I must have missed the front door." Lisa recomposed herself, letting a soft smile frame her features.

"I see," Iris said.

Lisa looked like a fox caught in a trap. She fiddled with her necklace, black stone glinting as her nails clicked across the surface.

Iris smiled, she knew that charm. She pulled, cleaned, and craved the tooth herself. It did best when fed on promises and blood. Lisa, whether she knew it or not, had been in contact with the fae before. She went from a nuisance, to a useful possibility. "Come along then." She led them to the front door, taking the first cement porch step, her left hip throbbed. Iris frowned.

"Are you alright?" Lisa asked.

"Old bones," she said. The screen door squeaked as she opened to let the girl in.

"My grandmother used to say she could feel storms brewing in her joints. I imagine it's quite painful," Lisa stood aside letting Iris pass.

"Would you like some tea?" Iris asked. "Or something to nibble on?"

"No, thank you. I can't stay long." Lisa still stood near the door, as if the carpet in Iris's living room was toxic.

Iris sat down on the wing chair with the view of the front yard. She scratched her fingers on the upholstery waiting for Lisa to speak. She took a deep breath. Lisa smelled like The Hag, a mix of honey and pale ale. Then again whenever The Hag was on the property, the smell of her seemed to ooze and leak through everything.

"I was coming by to see if you would be willing to switch shifts next Saturday." Lisa clasped her hands in front of her, to keep from fidgeting.

"You could've called," Iris said. "Not that I mind the company." She straightened up in the chair as if preparing to hold court.

"I was walking by and thought there would be no harm in me dropping in," Lisa dropped her hands and was now playing with the cord that held her pendant. "I thought I saw John pass by."

"Oh?" Iris asked. The wrinkles around her eyes creased as she smiled. The girl was fishing for information, and a terrible liar.

"I've seen him with my landlord once or twice. She rents rooms out every once in a while," Iris said. Whether they were supernatural or human they never had to pay rent, because they never lasted the month. Lisa however, didn't need that piece of information. "Please, take a seat." Iris gestured to a faded forest green couch.

Lisa walked over.

Iris ignored the fact that the girl left her shoes on. The last thing she wanted was the muck from outside on her carpets.

When Lisa sat down, the couch squeaked. "John would live here?" Lisa asked. "With her?" Her lips pursed and she crossed her arms over her chest.

"I wouldn't worry. I have trouble keeping track of the different suitors that come calling," Iris said. "None of them stick around for long." She smiled, Lisa shifted again in her seat and tugged at the edge of her white blouse. She clasped her hands on her lap again trying to still them.

Agnes acted a bit like this when she first started dating Connor. Suspicious of anyone that held more than a moment of his time. On top of her having the charm, Iris now knew what Lisa wanted. "To be honest, I'd rather see John end up with someone more like you," Iris smiled and sighed. "Sarah is nice enough, but I always thought you'd be a better match."

Lisa frowned at the mention of John's girlfriend. Something about that made Iris's cheek twitch. A secret, or loyalty to her friend? She used to be able to know the truth of a matter by a glance. What she wouldn't give to have the full strength of the fae again.

Best to take a gamble on the classic, jealousy. "He certainly has no business living here, let alone being tempted by my landlord."

"Tempted?" Lisa asked, eyes wide and fingers clenched the tooth.

Iris tapped the arm of her chair. "If she were to take a fancy to him. Then all it would be is a matter of time, especially if they were living in close quarters. The landlady always seems to go through a phase of infatuation with her renters." She flicked her hand as if she were discussing something as benign as grass growing. "However, John always seemed like a good lad. I'm sure his eyes would never wander."

"Sarah broke up with John," Lisa leaned back, her shoulders slumped.

Iris almost pitied the girl. "Oh. So he may be seeking some creature comfort."

Lisa's fingers once again wrapped around the charmed tooth. "I don't think John is like that."

"No, of course not," Iris had sown enough discontent in Lisa's mind about The Hag and John. "Interesting bauble you have there," Iris said. "How did you come by it?"

"Found it," The ridge of Lisa's fingernail clipped along the edges carved into the charm.

Iris stood up with a small groan and sat down next to Lisa on the couch. "I haven't seen one of those in years." She could feel the power tingling off the tooth. Normally, the tooth would act as a boon, enhancing the natural skills of the fae. This poor thing felt starved for promises but overfed on blood. Iris felt as if she would drown in the pain that now scorched through her. Her joints locked up and her breathing grew shallow. What had this girl done?

"Iris?" Lisa asked. "You know what it is?

Iris reached for the tooth. She had to get it away. "I used to make them. May I?"

Lisa pulled the necklace from around her neck and placed it in Iris' hands. It felt as if spirals of flames wrapped around her fingers and up into her wrist. "It's amazing. It hasn't cracked."

"You know how it works?" Lisa turned her full attention to Iris.

"Yes. But I don't think you do," Iris wrapped her long fingers around the tooth, some of her knobby knuckles popped as she gripped the poor thing. It needed a good cleaning and a heap of promises. The charm needed them like humans need water.

"You'd be surprised what you can find out by trial and error." Lisa glanced askance, then away from her. Lisa's gaze came back and fixated on the pendant. Her left hand now moving with a gentle tremble.

"Lisa, this really needs a good cleaning," Iris said. "I'd be happy to do that for you."

"I'd rather not be without it," Lisa held out her hand.

Iris pursed her lips, but gave it back. She would find another way to reclaim the abused piece. That did not mean she couldn't help bring some balance to the poor thing. Iris placed her hand on Lisa's shoulder. "You've fed it plenty of blood. What it really needs now is promises."

Lisa stood up and put the necklace back on. "You don't feed jewelry, Iris." She flounced towards the front door.

"This piece, you do," Iris said. "Let's try it together." She stood and walked over to the girl. Took her by the hand and wrapped the other around the tooth. "I promise to help keep an eye on my land-lord and John." One of the spiraled curls on the carving lightened to a stormy gray.

"Don't do that." Lisa pulled away from her. "When the color shifts I have to soak it again."

"The core of the tooth should look like onyx, the carvings on the outside should all be crystal clear," Iris said. "Since you've had it, have the carvings always been dark?"

"This was how I found it," Lisa hid the carving inside her shirt. "You keep saying tooth. What kind?"

"Not my place to tell. But if you change your mind about me giving it a clean. I could give you a few tips on how it works." Iris reached for the door handle. This felt like a bit of a sticky wicket. As much as she would like to yank the tooth from around the girl's spindly neck, patience would be best. The tooth only knew blood while with Lisa. It produced massive amounts of strength, more than a human should be able to handle.

"I'll keep that in mind," Lisa fled out the door and up the drive.

Iris shut the door and turned the deadbolt with a click. That was more than enough company for one day. A rapping on the door startled her. "Angels above and demons below. Who is it now?"

"Good morning, Iris." The police officer from the night before stood on her front porch.

14

WHAT LIES BENEATH

John walked in the door and braced himself for the inevitable weirdness of a house filled with centuries of memories. A clock ticked away on the wall of the small room. White paneled walls boxed him in, and a gray loveseat sat in the corner. A dark wooden door to his right with an iron handle seemed as innocuous as could be.

The only menacing thing he could see was a woodcarving that glared at him from the wall. It looked as if someone took the claws of a bird, the body of an eel, and the face of a man, and squished them all together. The mouth gaped open, and the tongue hung out. Large eyes made with abalone shells sparkled, catching the light from the miniscule window on the other wall. Another similar door stood in front of him, while a long shelf ran to the left of the door covered in lucky cats and other talismans. Above every entryway, an iron horseshoe nailed facing up.

A dripping sound came from somewhere behind the hall door. "Huh, it's not that weird," John said.

"What were you expecting?" Lilith's eyes darted around the room, while she rested her hands on her hips.

"I'm not sure," he said. All the eyes of the talismans in the room fixated on him and the back of his neck prickled as if something

99

else watched just out of sight. He took a couple of steps further into the room, trying to shake the feeling.

Lilith ran both her hands through her hair, scratching at the base of her neck. "Tell me the rules," she said.

"Stay with you," John said. "Don't touch anything and don't talk to anything."

Lilith grabbed him, pulling him back into the entryway. "Not even the walls. I mean it."

"Right, not even the walls. Even though they seem pleasant enough," John said chuckling at his joke. "Are you going to tell me why?"

Lilith grimaced and then yelled at the ceiling, "Connor!"

"What?" a call came back out of the dark-brown air grate above them.

"Your house talks?" John asked. He inched back to the front door.

"You should hear the toilet sing," a gruff tinkling voice replied. Like car keys pulled out of a pocket. Could tinkling be gruff? In this case, yes.

"Be quiet," Lilith said. "Don't interrupt." She stared up at the vent. "I have a guest. He is under my protection, understood?"

"Remember our deal, Hag," Connor said.

Iris had called Lilith the same thing at the plasma center. "Your house is rude," John wondered if anything else in the room would start talking.

"Shut up," Lilith said. "Alright Connor, anything to tell me?"

"Yea, the nasties in the loo are getting out of hand," he said.

Someone else giggled in the vent.

Lilith put her face into her gloved hands and let out a long breath. "Great."

"Also fights are coming up, and we want to watch 'em," Connor said. "Seems only fair with you imprisoning us and all."

"Alright," Lilith rolled her eyes. "I may join you, for the fights."

John could've sworn he heard a collective cheer at the agreement to the fights.

"And when you say the nasties?" Lilith asked.

"I mean the three that were left to their own devices since you put them in the hole," Connor said. "If you'd let us into the yard we may have been able to do something about that."

"I'd have to figure out how to define the yard," Lilith replied, picking at the scab nearest her hair line.

"Come on, Hag. You let us collect the mail. We can be trusted," Connor said. "You, not so much."

"Careful," Lilith said. "I could've sworn I took care of the tank the last time I passed through."

John watched Lilith banter with the ceiling. It seemed more like a landlord dealing with a tenant than an immortal chatting with a fairy.

"The last time you gave them any notice was when you moved them in," Connor said.

John moved away from the door and headed closer to the vent.

Lilith planted a hand on his chest and pushed him back. She shook her head, warning him not to come closer.

"I'll add them to my list," she said. "Anything else?"

"Nope," Connor said.

Lilith watched the vent, as if trying to discern a fortune from tea leaves. "Alright then. Remember, our deal, Connor."

"Always, Hag."

"And remind the rest of the clan." She opened the door, which groaned, and motioned to John to follow her. "Come on then."

On the right, Lilith entered through a narrow wooden door. A long workbench cluttered with mounds of papers and odd-looking bits of machinery stretched the length of the room, while antique tools hung from nails on the wall. Some rusted from age and neglect. They checked in, but could never leave.

John came up behind Lilith and looked over her shoulder. She took a knee and lifted a plastic cover from over a round hole in the ground. Dark water slished and sloshed inside.

"Why do you have a sump?" he asked.

Lilith handed him the lid, and he placed it on the workbench.

"This area used to be agricultural," she said. "Beautiful fragrant fruit orchards for miles." Her nose wrinkled.

John's nostrils were assaulted by a nasty, musty, damp smell.

"All of those trees used a lot of water and what didn't get used would run off and hit the foundation of the house. The sump keeps the basement from having water issues." Shifting her boot, it grounded it on the concrete floor. Standing up, she brushed the dust from her jeans. "It really shouldn't be this high."

"That's what, a foot?" he asked.

"No, my sump pit runs a little deeper than that," biting her bottom lip she looked to be trying to solve an equation. Pointing to her side, she said, "Hand me that yardstick."

John reached over to the tool bench and handed her the wooden stick.

Watching as Lilith stuck the stick down into the pit, her arm disappearing below the water line. "Ow!" Lilith yelped pulling her arm out of the water. It was covered in circular marks that had already scarred. The yardstick was no more, frayed fragments that looked like a paintbrush that had seen a year of use at daycare.

John moved back. Bracing against the workbench. "What was that?"

"Nemas," Lilith said dropping the frayed remains of the yardstick into the sump. "They are supposed to be managing the refuse from the house and nowhere near the sump."

John took a deep breath, drawn towards the hole that plunged into the ground. The black water rippled and burped. John's reflection warping in the unsteady water. "How did you end up with so many?"

Lilith picked up the sump cover and put it over the hole. She sat on the one clear space on the workbench, resting her hand on her chin. "Let's see. When I moved them into the tank, there were only three." Massaging her cheek, she continued to look puzzled till her eyes light up. "When they ended up in the tank they got a steady stream of food and nothing to attack them."

"That doesn't explain how you ended up with so many," John said.

"Now that I think about it, they normally only meet up to mate," Lilith looked over at him and gave him a sheepish grin.

"So you think they've been breeding?" John a hand through his hair.

"It's probably been a big old orgy since I stuck them down there." Lilith got up off the workbench knocking a loose screw, which clattered on the floor. "I better do something about that."

John looked down at the warped cover. "What happens if you don't?"

"The nest will burst," she said over one shoulder.

"And?" John felt like he was trying to pull information out of a reluctant child.

"They'll start eating anything that'll decompose."

A gurgle came from the sump.

John's jaw dropped.

Lilith was looking up at the ceiling as if recalling something. "The last time I saw a nemas nest burst, a village disappeared."

"What happens to all the nemas?" he asked.

"They ate until they exploded," she said. "Oh, if that happens, don't touch the remains."

"Why?"

"There tends to be an excess of stomach juices and, it'll melt your flesh," Lilith smiled. "Come to think of it, not the best idea to put more than one in the septic tank."

"Then why did you?" John leaned back on the workbench. Piles of letters looked more like mulch than correspondence. His hand shifted and sunk in the mail. On top of the heap, he noticed a large parchment envelope sitting as if it was king of the hill. A red wax logo with two crossed sickles marked it like a fresh scrape on a knee.

"I couldn't be bothered killing them all," she said.

"Or you could've just pumped the tank like anyone else," John said.

"Never having to pump the tank seemed like a great idea." Lilith looked over at him like she expected him to agree. "At the time. Come on. I need to check my journals." She got off the bench and walked out the door.

"Where are we going?" John followed Lilith down the hall.

"The water height makes me nervous," she said.

On the right, another door looked like a giant cat had taken to using it as a scratching post. A large iron bar across the middle kept it shut. At the end, a plain brown door stood. John followed Lilith into the room on the left.

"The kitchen?" John asked passing a stacked washer and dryer, an empty sink, and clean counters. A whirring sound came from his right, and he headed towards the fridge. "Odd place to keep journals."

"I don't keep them in the kitchen," Lilith said looking back at John. "Oh, don't open the fridge."

"Why?" John asked pulling his hand back.

"Journals first," Lilith said walking past the stove and towards the door of the cold storage. "Unspeakable horrors, later." Pulling the door open, the old hinges groaned like an old man with indigestion.

"That's not ominous." John walked in after her. Shivering as he entered the dark, dank space.

With a click, a lone yellow bulb lit up rows of shelves covered in bottles and cans. Pickled fruits and vegetables, all of which looked more like alien experiments than consumables. Once bright with color, they were now a dull shade of tan-ish.

Lilith tore at a piece of sheetrock on the wall. She grunted as she put a boot on it and pried at the panel.

"Would you like some help?" he asked.

"Would it involve you touching something?"

"Yes."

"No." She stumbled back, loose sheetrock in her hand. Revealing a wall of rocks, another security feature. Lilith pushed and prodded at the rocks, which tumbled out of sight, the yellow light piercing into the darkness she revealed. Dirt, roots, and rocks made up the walls, and slate gray stairs descended out of sight. She disappeared into the dark and then for her next trick, made an unlit torch appear in her place. "Go use the stove and light that."

"I have permission to touch the stove?" John took the torch from her hand.

"Yes," she said. Heavy boots thudded down the stairs. "Don't burn my house down!" Her voice became distant. "Now, hurry up."

John ran out to the stove, turned the dial causing a methodical click, then a blue flame jumped out of the burner. He held the darkened cloth on the end of the torch over the flames. Black plumes rose off the fabric like wisps of midnight sky followed by vibrant yellow and reds flames.

John headed back into the cold storage, the torch flames casting strange shadows through the bottled goods. He headed for the hole in the wall and descended the slate staircase. Fire sizzling in the dark brought carvings out on the dirt walls. Extensive, intricate swirled patterns that morphed into things with teeth and claws. *Glad I haven't run into something like that,* he thought.

Light blue rock marbled with white appeared a few steps further along the walls of the tunnel, opening up into a grand chasm. A scuttle caused John to hold the torch out. *It's only Lilith. Right?* The air grew chill and damp as he descended lower into the chasm-like room.

"Took you long enough," Lilith called. "Bring that light over, would you?"

John walked forward and stopped as Lilith rammed herself against a large stone door. A small scraping sound was her reward. "You could help," she said, her face contorting in pain. She rubbed the arm she used as a battering ram.

"You told me not to touch anything," John said.

"In the house," Lilith said. "Are we in the house?"

"No? I suppose not?" John headed over torch in hand, putting his back to the door his shoulders scrunched up in the cold, together they moved the door a couple of feet and slipped in.

Lilith grabbed the torch from John, lighting two lanterns hanging by chains near the door. Flames climbed up the chain, with a crackle and pop, followed by the smell of heated metal. A chandelier high on the vaulted ceiling lit, connected to a complex web of chains that knitted all the fixtures together.

The fire raced from chain to chain till the hall blazed in the light. Stone shelves filled with rows and rows of leather-bound books appeared out of the darkness with each new lit fixture. John's jaw dropped at the immensity of it all.

"You'll catch flies if you leave your mouth hanging open." Lilith smirked, putting the torch in a holder by the door. Turning around, she headed down the hall towards a large wooden desk.

John's foot kicked a rock, which skittered and fell into a long gash in the stone. In the middle of the floor, just in front of the huge desk, a skull of a giant lizard-like creature loomed. The brow bone came up to John's waist. The jawline stuck in a permanent smile. Front fangs jutted out and behind them, a line of shorter curved dagger-like teeth caught the glow of the lights. The skull was not complete, gaps in the tooth line appeared purposeful, likes books missing from a shelf.

John skirted around the skull, standing between it and the desk. He caught a blue flicker out of the corner of his eye. "What is that?" Jon turned back to the skull, to see it better.

Lilith standing at the desk replied, "Dragon skull." The gentle ruffle of pages stopped.

"Dragon?" John took a few steps towards the skull. "Where do you find a dragon?" he asked.

"You don't," Lilith said. She slammed the book closed. "They're all gone."

"Why?" John asked.

"I killed them all." She frowned, shifting the book on the table, aligning and straightening leatherworking tools. "And a good thing, too," she said. "In this hall, you can look, touch, and read whatever you want."

"What is all this?" John rifled through some of the yellow parchment on the desk in front of him.

"My records," she said as if busy remembering something. She pulled her journal from her pocket and scribbled a note.

A dark wooden box at the corner of her desk pulled his attention, the same logo of the crossed sickles etched in the lid. He lifted the lid. Lilith slammed her hand on top, closing it before he could see inside.

"Except that," she said. "Things sometimes have a way of rearranging themselves down here." She pulled it across the desk towards her. Parchment scattered as she tugged it closer. "This belongs in another hallway."

"What's in it?" John asked.

"An old skull." She picked it up and cradling it to her chest. As they walked down the hall, the stone shelves loomed over them. Packed with tomes wrapped in black, silver, blue, red and green all mixed together some of them so brilliant they stood out like stars in a clear night sky.

"I don't know if I could read any of these," he said. The floor tiles lay cross-hatched with scratches up and down like an art student that had started a shading project but left it unfinished. Ahead a large stone door appeared, carved in spirals.

"This hall is in English, or at least the journals I started writing in English, the ones I collected from others, maybe not." Lilith focused on the door ahead of her.

John paused at a shelf, pulling a journal off and opening it. Faded scribbles made up the left page, and a drawing on the right looked like a jackalope with fangs. "Do you have a copy of these somewhere?"

"This is it," she said.

"You should digitize these," he slid the book back into place. "It'd take up less space."

"I'm not worried about space." Lilith placed the box in a gap, between volumes on one of the last shelves.

"It'd be searchable," John rubbed his chin. "How is this even organized, anyway?"

"Chronologically. I think," Lilith crossed her arms, leaning on the bookcase. "I have no intention of sharing this with the general public."

"Aren't you worried about it getting damaged?" The quiet of the vast cavern swallowing his voice.

"You ask a lot of questions," Lilith grabbed a ladder, lining it up near one of the lit chandeliers that crackled above. She pulled a journal off a lower shelf. The ladder creaked as she climbed upward, leaning back towards the flames.

"What are you doing?" he asked worried both that she might fall, and that she was too close to the flame.

The book caught alight. Lilith looked down, smiled, and dropped it at his feet.

He yelled jumping back from the flames, then trying to stomp the fire out before Lilith joined him, ending the fire a heavy thump from her boot. She picked the journal up and handed it to him. Warm to the touch, it felt like a lizard that soaked up too much sun, but the pages were undamaged.

"How did you manage that?" He turned the journal over in his hands.

"Dragon skin." Lilith smiled. "Amazing stuff, even helps me remember the content."

"Go on," John said.

She shrugged, shoving her hands deep into her jean pockets. "Without it, I wouldn't be able to remember more than a lifetime."

John opened the book, flipping the pages. All were scorch-free.

"Supernatural creatures can use and manipulate certain types of energies. Dragonskin protects and enhances memory." Lilith took the book from him and put it back on the shelf. "As long as the paper is inside the leather, the memories will stay. The real problem is theft."

She hoisted the box back into her arms like a mother picking up a child. "I made a deal with a fairy clan who handles that."

"There is a whole clan?" John asked, casting about for them.

"Yep. That rude little voice in the air-duct happens to be Connor. The head of the clan that protects my house." Carrying the box, she headed for the stone door at the end of the hall. "I broke protocol by bringing you in unannounced."

"I don't see what keeps them from coming down here anyway." John looked around expecting something or someone to fly off the shelf at him. He inspected the large carved arches above. "Can they hear us?"

"No, this is not the house." They passed through the next archway. "This is something else." Lilith drummed her fingers on the box. "It's where I keep all my journals and some odds and ends. The only entrance is through the house."

"Why not let them have free run down here?" John asked, taking a step over a large gash in the floor. "I doubt they could do any real damage."

"Forget what Tinkerbell taught you about fairies," Lilith said, picking up the pace, the thud of her boots echoing down the hall.

"What are they going to do? Sprinkle me with pixie dust?" He flitted his hand in the air with an imaginary wand.

Lilith stopped and turned on him. "Fairies are quick, clever, and strong," she said. "Oh, bonus they have access to magic, where all they have to do is speak and things, bad things, happen to you." She took a breath, seeming to settle herself. "Don't speak to them. They'll twist your words and use them against you. Fairies are big on semantics."

"Why did they call you a hag?" he asked.

Lilith started walking again. "It's a term of endearment."

"Lilith, your real name seems like less of an insult," John said.

"The fairies are not allowed to use it," she said. "Part of the contract."

"Why not?" John asked trotting to catch up.

"Names have power," Lilith said. The box cradled in her arms rattled. "'ll try not to use your name in the house. I wouldn't let it slip if it were you."

"But you know their names?" John asked.

"Yep," she said. "Helps keep the lot of them in line."

"Cool, you have a fairy army." John rubbed his hands together.

Lilith's brow scrunched up. "No, I don't." Shaking her head she went on, "You have to be specific. They'll turn it on you, for kicks. The contract to guard the house is about six inches thick and took me a week to write out."

"They'll keep a contract?" John scratched at some flaky skin on his elbow.

"Yep," she said, "and then do just about anything to get out of it."

"Where is it?" John asked.

"I keep it down here for safety, bound in iron," she said. "They'd run amok if they weren't bound to the property. Fairies aren't keen on staying in one place for too long." They reached the door carved in spirals. "Pull that open for me."

John grabbed the ring on the door. "How long have they been stuck?" he grunted as he pulled on the massive iron ring.

"They've been tied to the property give or take four hundred years," Lilith said.

The door gave way, the bottom scraping against the ground which sounded like an old forgotten chant. John leaned against it, catching his breath. "Why didn't they do something about the nemas?"

"Not in the contract," Lilith said. A broad beam of flickering light from the hall guided her steps. The sizzle and crackle of the fire above came down like someone whispering a secret in your ear. Identical boxes to the one Lilith held lined the shelf. She ran her hand over the box and sighed.

John rubbed his shoulder unwilling to enter.

He felt like an intruder. This space was quiet, sacred even. Lilith came back out and joined him.

"What are we going to do about the nemas?" John asked.

"We?" Lilith raised a brow. "We, do nothing." She rubbed her face, fingertips pulling at the bottom of her eyes making her look ghoulish. "I go dig up the entrance to the septic tank."

"I can help dig," John helped close the heavy door before walking back towards the main entrance.

"Why?" Lilith asked. The chains creaked above them. "No need to get your hands dirty."

"I have friends and an ex I'm trying to win back that live around here. If the nemas get out they would be in some real trouble." Another flicker of blue pulled John's attention. Again it had come from the dragon skull.

"Whether I want to admit it or not, they are my responsibility," Lilith said. "Instead of mucking about with the septic tank, you could read." Lilith pulled one of the books off the shelf. "Tomes of information down here." She opened it flipping the pages. The whisper of their movement like moths fluttering in the dark. "Aren't you a tad curious about what's in the books?"

"I don't know if I want to read what's down here," John said. "Feels a little odd reading someone's journal. But I would like to meet Connor." John's shoulder itched, he scratched at a patch of scaly skin.

Lilith returned to her desk, book in hand. She started making piles out of the loose paper. Thick dark red thread and scraps of leather littered the desk. "No," she said. "Bad idea."

John joined her. He picked up a piece of silver leather, turning it over in his hand. It squeaked as he pushed it between his fingers. "The sickle logo on the box, what's it from?" John asked.

"It's from a very old cult." Lilith traced a circle on the desk as if recreating the design.

"There was a letter upstairs with that mark," he said. "Does that mean they are still around?"

"Where upstairs?" Lilith asked. She dropped the stack of papers, and they fluttered to the floor.

"On the bench in your office," John said.

"Bloody hell." Lilith jumped into action, moving out from behind the desk and heading towards the door. "Come on!" She tugged on a dark rope hanging by the lanterns.

John blinked, and darkness engulfed them.

"I'm going to murder that fairy," Lilith said. The flame of the torch disappearing up the stairs. "Close that door would you."

John tugged and struggled with the door to the entrance of the halls. It grated on the floor a couple of feet. *Good enough.* John didn't want to be left in the dark. He ran up the stairs towards the light. "What's the big deal?

"Connor broke the contract," she said.

Lilith rushed through the hole she'd torn in the wall.

Plaster hit John in the face. Coughing, he came out of the cold storage. Lilith stubbed the torch out with her boot and dumping it in the sink. She then raced ahead, running into the office and coming back out. She yelled at the ceiling, "Connor, you've broken our deal!"

Bits of ceiling tile came down in a blizzard of white. John leaned in the doorway across from the office. Lilith clawed at the ceiling like a raccoon.

"Have I now?" Connor asked from the vent. "Name it."

Lilith covered in plaster dust snarled. She pulled the letter out of her pocket. "This is important," she said. "I asked if anything important arrived."

"You did," Connor said. "That letter has no bearing on me or mine, so it is not important to me."

"He's got you there." John looked up at the vent. He liked that Connor stood his ground against Lilith.

"Good lad," Connor said. "I like this one."

"You know what I meant," Lilith said. She opened the office door, slamming the letter and her journal down on the workbench. "You don't talk." She waggled a finger in John's face, then returned her attention to the vent.

John stifled a chuckle. He leaned on a door behind him, and something inside gurgled. Turning around, he opened the door. John fumbled for the light switch, then found it and flicked it on. A white toilet positioned in front of a shower with a frosted glass door. The space so tight it made John wondered if you could sit down without hitting your knees. *Why does every other room in this house look like a hallway?* The shower started to gurgle again, probably meant the line had a clog, or something worse, since it was Lilith's house.

"Get out of there," Lilith said.

"Your tank may be overflowing," John said. "I thought the Nemas ate the waste?"

"They do." She heading back into the hall. "It's not clogged with waste." Lilith's boots crunched over the scattered plaster on the floor. "Connor, fix the ceiling. Also, the house will be in peril if any of the nemas climb up from the tank." She started walking back down the hall towards the front room. "You know what to do."

"You may want to be more specific," John said. Still in the bathroom, watching the drain. "Just because he knows what to do doesn't mean he or his clan will do it."

"Right," Lilith said. "Kill all the nemas in the house and on the property."

A honeyed voice came from the bathroom cabinet, "Don't trust her." He opened the cabinet hoping to catch a glimpse of who spoke. An array of glass bottles sat on the middle shelf along with a half-used tube of toothpaste.

John glanced back into the hall. Lilith and Connor were exchanging obscenities.

"Why?" he asked the empty room.

"She is dangerous," another soft voice came from the toilet tank. Hefting the lid, he found only the float ball and chain bobbing in the water.

"No kidding," John said. The lid grounded against the tank as he put it back.

"She is friend to no creature," this voice echoed out of the shower drain. John stared down the dark hole, still seeing nothing.

"All are meat," this voice, higher and more feminine came from the faux wooden vanity. John opened the door. Dark-blue glass glinted in the light, the bottles tinkling as John moved them. A clatter behind him made him jump.

"You gopher loving, cricket eating, elderberry consuming, tart fished, tongue-tied, son of an impotent gnome!" Lilith started clawing at the ceiling, again.

"Look out!" The voice cried from the cabinet.

A rumble rolled beneath his feet. Chunks of tile crackled, and porcelain rained down on him, the toilet was no more. Water cascaded out of the wall. A writhing mass of sleek black coils burst out of the hole where the toilet had been.

John stumbled out of the bathroom both disgusted and interested in what a nemas was.

Lilith jumped in, blade in hand, slashing away at the tendrils. Black goo splattered and hissed, causing the baby blue paint on the walls to peel.

John braced himself against the far wall of the office. Something landed on his shoulder, and he flinched as a terracotta blur darted into the bathroom.

The bathroom vent flew off the wall. Little figures flitted into the fray. A cyclone of fall colors filled the room. A bright orange streak took point, it must be Connor.

Connor stalked the tendrils. Every move fell another large coil. Flashes of yellow, red, and brown cutting down the unruly mass that grew out of the cracks in the floor.

"John! Get the torch!" Lilith ordered, hair matted to her face. A dark iridescent liquid seemed to melt and deform her features. She sliced at another segmented tube, the black ooze it sprayed hitting her arm.

John ran to the sink, grabbed the torch, and lighting it on the gas range. His sneaker sizzled when he stepped into the bathroom.

"Stop! Don't touch the ooze!" Lilith said, a mass of tendrils burst through the shower door, smashing Lilith against the other wall. "Connor," Lilith called from under the wriggling mass. "Call your clan back!"

Slipping out from under the writhing pile, she slid over to John. "Torch!" She reached out, the flesh of her fingers melted away, leaving only stark white bone.

John handed it over then moved back, and kicking off his melting sneaker. He pulled off a sock that also started to decompose before the goo got to his foot.

"Out!" Connor cried, hanging off the wall vent, pulling wobbling bits of light back into the duct.

"Ripped little man," John said squinting at the muscled figure inside the colored spark. A spiraled carving swung around his neck as he moved. Matching etched marks sprawled across his shoulders. Connor jumped into the vent. He hoisted the waist on his dark green trousers, rubbing at the short red Mohawk that crested his head.

"Not a wing to be seen," John said wishing he had a magnifying glass to examine him better.

Lilith slashed down the remaining tendrils then used the torch to burn the stubs. She twisted the torch in the drainpipe like she was putting out a cigarette. Clearwater continued to spill into the room from all the drains. She splashed through and yelled into the vent. "Connor kill the water main, would ya?" She put the now unlit torch down on the sink. Drenched in sludge, she began removing the nemas' remains from off herself. Angry red blisters formed weeping and scabbing. "I liked those tattoos," she sighed.

Lilith rinsed off in the water that slowed, yet still poured out of the busted pipe., taking its time come to a stop. The remaining liquid escaped down the drains and cracks in the floor, gurgling as it went.

"I'm going to murder that thing to death!" Lilith stormed out of the bathroom and down the hall.

"Hold on." John ran after her, the soggy carpet squishing under his sneakers.

"What?" she demanded, face still strangely asymmetrical.

"You may want to put some clothes on." John pointed.

Lilith looked down at her lack of shirt, semi-demolished jeans filled with a patchwork of singed holes and toeless boots, then shrugged.

John made a strangled noise, looking at the door to her right instead of the skin visible through her shirt.

"Fine," she said, pushing him out of the way.

John continued to avert his gaze as she passed.

She hoisted the metal bar off the door towards the end of the hall. John caught a glimpse of shelves covered in books. Some rustling and cursing, and a crash that didn't sound good echoed through the hall before she came back out in a fresh black shirt and pair of jeans, strangling a pair of boots in her hand. "I'm going to dig them up, and I'm going to bludgeon, stab, and beat them to death." She finished lacing up her boots, hopping on one foot while tying a double knot. "After that, I'm going to eat their weight in steak."

15

BLITZKREIG BOP

Lisa stomped up the gravel path. If John wanted to spend his time with some pale whore, that was his choice. She could find other entertainment. A white weathered shed framed by bare oak trees sat at the end of the path. Mike, long and lean, waved at her from the doorway while Mark disappeared inside. They were always good for a laugh, and Lisa could use a laugh.

Around the shed an empty field lay, nothing but scattered remains of corn stalks. Patches of ice that looked like broken glass littered the ground blazing white in the afternoon sun.

"Hey boys," Lisa said as she walked in. Mark struggled with a generator that coughed and sputtered as he tried to turn it over.

"Sup." Mike sprawled out on a dilapidated mustard-yellow couch, feet resting on a makeshift coffee table. Made of a bit of particle board and two wooden crates, it appeared less than sturdy.

"You know, you really shouldn't park so close to the shed," Mark gave up on the generator and flopped down on a ragged green recliner, the material flecked with tan speckles.

Lisa raised a brow. "I didn't."

"Yeah. Lisa can actually manage to walk down the road and not end up like you, Puff," Mike said, a half-grin pulled across his face.

"Were you followed?" Mark asked.

Lisa rolled her eyes. Mark seemed on edge, paranoid. "Started without us, did you?" she asked.

"No," Mark said. "I thought we may be having other company."

Too bad, no Sarah for you. Lisa thought. "Sorry to disappoint, but it'll only be me tonight."

"Oh, I thought you'd bring your friend along," Mike said. He shifted on the couch rusty springs squeaking beneath the fabric. "Is it a good idea to leave her alone at the moment?"

"What are you talking about?" Mark picked at the loose fibers on the chair, tearing the polyester.

"John and Sarah broke up," Lisa said. "It was messy." She cringed at the thought of the strange woman naked on John's bed.

"We should go get her then," Mark sat up in the recliner. It groaned in protest.

"No," Lisa folded her arms across her chest.

"Come on. A little fun will do her good." Mike's sneaker scraped across the particle board as he pulled his feet off the table.

"You can't," Lisa's eyes narrowed at Mike.

"Why not? Mike missed the warning in her voice, instead scratching at his arm as if uncomfortable under her glare. A field mouse who became aware of the red-tailed hawk circling above him.

"You just can't," Lisa sat down on the couch. Leaning forward, she fiddle with the loose sheets of rolling paper on the table. They crinkled beneath her fingers as she balled some up in her fist.

Mike turned and grinned at her. Then put his arm around her shoulder, giving it a squeeze. "But, the more the merrier-"

Lisa scowled. "Drop it."

"Yeah, man. It's not like she's dead," Mark leaned back in the recliner, staring at the ceiling.

Lisa shook his arm off and stood up. "Do you really want to be the rebound?" she asked. "Or worse, that pesky guy who can't take a hint?"

"No," Mike hung his head, resting his pointed chin on his hands.

"I'd wait," Mark said. "I'm sure you'll have other chances."

Lisa laughed. *That's what you think.*

"What?" Mike asked. "I've got a chance."

"Why? Because you've said more than three words to her?" Mark asked. He pulled at his knitted yellow and orange hat with an orange pom pom on top. "The less people who know about the shed, the better. What we are doing in here isn't exactly legal."

"Yeah, but it's not exactly illegal," Mike shrugged his shoulders.

Lisa paced near the door like a caged leopard. "I agree with Mark on this one."

"Sarah wouldn't tell anyone," Mike said.

"Especially if she doesn't know," Lisa cocked her head.

Mike gave a sheepish grin and scratched at the top of his head. "Well-"

"You told her? When?" Lisa asked.

"A while ago," Mike said. "Sarah seemed interested. She didn't think John would be cool with it."

"If she knew," Lisa sighed, "John knows." She clicked her nail on her teeth.

"Oh," Mike sunk back in to the couch, dejected. "That's not a good thing."

Mark bit at his bottom lip then said, "We may have to do something about that."

"I'll handle it," Lisa flicked her braid over her shoulder.

"I bet you will." Mike wagged his eyebrows at her. "Now that Sarah's no longer in the picture-"

"Isn't there some sort of code that you don't date your friend's exes?" Mark asked, his glazed look and owlish blinking not adding any intelligence points to his look.

"Sarah won't care," Lisa pulled her phone out and tapped the screen. John still hadn't responded to her messages.

"She's on shift with me tonight, anyway," Mike said. "If she happens to tag along after work, you guys wouldn't mind, right?" Mike stood up and dusted off his jeans.

Mark said, "If John is shift-manager, and the break up is as bad as Lisa says, she may not be at her shift."

"I'd be willing to bet on it," Lisa crossed her arms, smiling.

"Is John shift-manager tonight?" Mike hit his own forehead with a smack. "Really don't want to get chewed out for missing my last shift."

"I covered for you," Mark said. He squinted his eyes as if trying to remember what he said. "I think. That whole night is a little squiggly."

"You were high at work?" Lisa asked.

"And you were worried about me." Mike showed unbrushed teeth, bits of unknown substances poking out between them.

"No." Mark said. "There was some weird gray woman, that ran off with John." He rubbed at his temples and groaned a little. "Maybe, I was high."

Lisa frowned. Her, again. *She is getting to be a huge problem.* She thought. Her hand went for her pendant, which had tinges of blue on the edges of the carving. It reminded her of blue skies cracking through gray storm clouds. She looked over at Mike. "You better get going, if you don't want to be late."

"Hot date and all." Mike winked at Lisa as he headed for the shed door.

"She won't be there," Lisa waited for Mike to open the door.

"I bet you she will," Mike stood up taller, as if that gave him any credibility. "In fact, if she isn't, I'll buy dinner."

Lisa smiled. This was a bet she couldn't lose. "Dinner for everyone?"

"I'm liking the sound of this," Mark said.

"Good," Mike pulled on the shed door which creaked as it opened. "Because I could really use a ride to work."

Mark rolled his eyes and got out of the recliner. "Come on, then."

The trio walked out of the whitewashed shed.

"We will come back later and eat," Lisa said. "In fact, I feel like steak. What about you, Mark?"

"Steak is good," Mark said. He wrapped the chain through the handles on the door, sliding the shackle of the lock through the chain. It closed with a clink.

"Good thing you'll be paying, Lisa." Mike threw his arms around Mark and her.

That's what you think. Lisa loved being right.

16

SLY AS A FOX

Would you like to come in, Officer?" Iris asked the young man standing on her front porch. He smelled like the memory of something gone bad, but she couldn't quite remember what. Maybe Connor knew something.

"Thanks, but please, call me Zech," he said. "I have a few follow up questions about last night's events."

Zech. I know that name. She thought. *From where?* The screen door rattled as it closed behind him. Iris closed the front door and shuffled back to her wingback chair.

"We've been trying to get a hold of the shift manager at the plasma center." Zech stood in front of a white-painted brick fireplace. He flipped open a notebook, pages rustling as he turned them. "John, is the name I have listed."

An air duct rattled. A whisper came from Connor, "Mum, be careful. That's a bloody angel and I think it's the one that runs around with The Hag."

Iris gulped and then smiled. "Yes, dear."

"Get him out of here," Connor hissed.

"Excuse me?" Zech asked.

"Don't mind me." Iris adjusted her hands and laid them in her lap. "John is here with my landlady. She's taken quite the fancy to him." She pulled a loose flaxen strand of hair and tucked it behind her ear. "Always feels a little odd when she has guests around."

Zech's brow furrowed. "Really? Is the interest mutual?"

"Not sure, to be honest," Iris couldn't believe the jealousy card would serve her twice today. She would have to be careful how she seasoned this tale. Best leave the details to the angel's imagination. "She rents out the top floor to me and uses the basement. Come to think of it, she only really comes around when she is entertaining someone."

Zech chewed on his bottom lip, and closed the notebook with a snap.

"Is everything alright?" Iris asked. "The center is all cleaned up and we've had no complaints from any of the donors."

"Everything is fine," Zech tugged at the neckline of his black sweater.

Iris nodded, fine in this context must mean something is not fine.

"You don't mind if I go down and have a word with your land lady?" he asked.

"Anything to help the investigation," Iris said. "I just hope you don't interrupt anything."

"Me too," Zech yanked the front door then the screen door open, storming out of the house.

"Mum, are you mad?" Connor asked from the duct.

"No." She got out of her seat and headed to the kitchen. Pleased as a cat that caught a starling.

"She's insane," Agnes's voice came from the sink drain. "The eternal stirrer, this one."

Iris turned the faucet on a short blast of water came out then stopped. A yelp came from the pipe.

"Were the water works necessary?" Agnes' voice now came from the air duct.

"If you feel the need to question my sanity and call names, then yes, I believe they were." Iris tapped a butter knife on the sink, looking out the kitchen window. She wondered if it would be another dry winter. She missed the snow.

"You need to stay away from The Hag's prey," Connor said.

"Which one, Zech or John?" she asked.

"Both!" the fairies in the vent cried in unison.

"You can't expect me to stand by and watch her devour another poor soul," Iris said.

"Callieach's wind! She can eat whoever she wants, as long as the clan stays safe," Connor said. "This isn't about the boy. You are after the contract."

"John will get the contract for us," Iris said.

"You have no words to use," Connor said. "What is it going to take for that to get through to you. You have nothing to barter or bargain."

Iris closed her eyes and took a deep breath. True, she didn't have magic, strength, or the youth that she once had. There was much to be said for strength beyond magic and she would be damned if she didn't use every tool she could get her hands on.

"There may be something else," Agnes said. "He has the sight."

Iris dropped the knife. It clattered in the sink. "We could find the others and the missing little one," Iris said. "All we need is freedom from the contract."

"Just because he can get it, doesn't mean he'd use it to help us," Connor said.

"Fool child," Iris said. "He is our chance. All we have to do is keep him alive."

"We'd have more luck collecting teeth from a hen," Connor sounded less than pleased.

Iris ignored him. "Did he glow, Agnes?"

"Blue," Agnes said. "True blue."

One of the few things that Iris and Agnes could agree on was finding the lost clans. Especially her only grandchild.

"Connor," Agnes said. "Please. Who knows when we'll get another chance."

"For once, we agree," Iris said.

The Hag appeared outside, on the patio. She stood over John with her arms crossed as he dug up one of the in-ground planters. "What on earth is going on out there? Did I miss something?"

"The nasties tried to take a bite or two out of The Hag," Connor said. "She plans on doing something about it."

"We have to keep that boy alive," Iris said. "Agreed?" She stared at the brown tile imagining that they were below her feet.

"No arguments from me," Agnes said.

"Alright," Connor caved. "I'll do what I can."

"Someone is trying to come in downstairs," Agnes voice faded away as she spoke.

"Probably that ruddy angel," Connor said. "Be careful, Mum." And he too was gone.

Looking back out the window, The Hag disappeared and John now stood topless shuddering in the cold. Iris shook her head in disapproval. *Too kind and too trusting this one.*

She walked over to the sliding door that lead out to the back patio. Grit and dirt scraping in the track as she opened it.

"John?" she called. "What are you doing out there? Without a shirt on, no less."

"I, uh-" John glanced at the hole in the ground.

"Helping the Hag?" Iris asked.

John nodded. "She needed something to use for a torch. My shirt seemed good enough," John said. "I liked that shirt."

Iris pulled her robe closer around her thin frame, shaking her head. She stepped out of the house and tiptoed over to the entrance of the septic tank. No smell. Not much of anything in the dank hole below. "Those little buggers have gotten big."

"You should have seen the one downstairs," John rubbed bare his arms.

"I imagine those are the ones that could fit through the pipes." Iris took a few steps back.

"They get bigger?" John moved to stand by her again.

"Yep," Iris said. "Glad I'm not down there." Iris stood for a moment and let the cold soak into her skin. "You've been downstairs then. Meet anyone?"

"Don't know if chatting with walls counts as meeting anyone," John said. "But I like Connor."

"How is he doing?" Iris asked. "I'd appreciate anything you can tell me."

"Seems good," John said. "He has a bit of a mouth on him."

The wrinkles around Iris's eyes crinkled as a sad smile crossed her face. "I miss them."

"You live in the same house," John said. "Don't they visit?"

"They would if they could, dear." Iris shrugged her shoulders.

"The contract?" John asked.

"That would be why," Iris said. "It'd be nice to see my family one more time, before I die."

"What would happen if the clan got the contract?" John asked.

"We'd leave," Iris said. "Take to the skies. I tried once before, but ended up like this." Iris stretched out a hand, the skin taut over her joints and rice-paper thin. I have no right to ask you, John but if you hear anything about the contract, would you let me know? The freedom of my family means everything to me."

John stared at the hole in the ground, a frown on his face. *Had she over done it?*

"If I tell you what I learn, I want a favor in return," John said.

"I can't make bargains on behalf of the clan," Iris said. "But I'm sure Connor would listen to me if I asked."

"The clan can't harm The Hag, me, or anyone I care about," John said. "Do you think they could manage that?"

"Is that all?" Iris asked. "No one can harm The Hag. She'd need a heart, for starters."

John glared at her. His blue eyes hard, with the gray skies behind, he looked as if the sky would cry if he demanded it.

Iris shuddered. There was something more than just fairy blood in this one. "Done," she said. "If Connor will listen to me."

"I haven't seen it, but I think the contract is downstairs in the third hall," John said. "I think we all need to find a way to work together."

Naive child, Iris thought. *There is no working with The Hag.*

John wiped his nose with the back of his hand.

"Let me see if I can find you a shirt," Iris said. "No sense standing out here and freezing." Iris headed inside, the warmth of the house enveloping her. She stared at the floor, deep beneath the house sat the contract, The Hag foolishly left it in the same place. The key to freedom.

17

DANSE MACABRE

Lilith felt a little bad that she left John shirtless in the yard, but something had to be done about the nemas. She rubbed at her neck, bits of glass stinging beneath her skin. *I really need to start keeping an eye on the creatures around here.* She took a few steps forward, the dark water seeping up the legs of her jeans. "Ugh," she walked forward into the first tank. The shaft of light from above was not enough to light her way any further.

Lilith checked one more time for gas, but couldn't smell anything.

The tank was too clean.

She wrapped John's t-shirt around the shovel, cracked open the lighter, and dumped the fluid on it, she flicked the flint and wheel causing it to spark. The fire crackled as it came to life. It wouldn't last long, but it would have to do.

Lilith smiled. John reminded her to make a note in her journal about what had been going on. She liked having the kid around. When was the last time she made a friend?

Smoke tickled her nose, bringing her back to the moment, and she coughed. She could figure out another way to get more dragon skin and keep him around.

She knew three tanks stretched ahead of her beneath the yard to break down the waste. Lilith built the septic system large, hoping it would mean less maintenance. The nest, if she had to guess, would be in the third section. *Better get moving, if the nemas don't get me, the lack of oxygen will.*

Lilith held the lit torch-shovel aloft. She took another step and something squirmed underfoot. Ramming the shovel into it, the movement stopped. She gasped for breath, continuing deeper into the darkness, the liquid now up to her waist. A gray cement wall rose in front of her, covered in cracks and flaking cement. Using the shovel like a battering ram she hit the wall until it burst. A slithering mass of tendrils flooded into the first tank.

John shuddered in the cold, watching the dead grass. He pictured Lilith wading through the tank. While he felt bad for the clan and Iris, there had to be a better way to handle the situation, or any of the other creatures for that matter. He kept watch, not that he could see anything to be alarmed about.

Snow falling on the mountain range caught his attention. He kept hearing about how terrible winters were in Utah, but he'd yet to see snowfall in the valley. Nothing like the wet Minnesota winters he grew up with, where the cold seeped in and didn't leave till spring road construction started.

Thunder rolling through the cloudless sky, distracting him like a passing train. The smell of sweet chili sauce drifted down and wrapped around him. It was intoxicating and seemed to permeate everywhere. Tall evergreens stretching up to the sky cutting off his view of the shopping complex. *I wonder if the smell came from over there.*

The cold pricked at his skin, like someone taking pins out of a sewing project and putting them in a pincushion. John, crossing his arms, began rubbing his skin to keep warm. *I hope Iris has a shirt I can use.*

"You know if you lose the pants and briefs I could arrest you for indecent exposure," The cop that questioned John before stood at the barb wire fence. He climbed over it like a bored cat, white hi-tops crunching across the grass as he came towards John.

"Excuse me?" John asked.

The officer, with hands in his pockets, and the long black sleeves of the same color as his sweater, made his arms disappear. *Man, I wish I had his sweater I'm starting to get cold.* John thought.

"Would you like my sweater?" The officer asked, pulling it off before John could answer and handing it over to him. "I won't take no for an answer. It's a little weird talking to you shirtless."

"Uh, thanks. Appreciate it." John pulled the sweater over his head. The smell of chili and vinegar overwhelming him, coughing at the smell, it seemed so strong he could taste it. "Thanks again," he said trying not to gag.

"Don't worry, the smell will fade." He walked towards the top of the tank where Lilith disappeared. Squinting into the darkness, he took a deep breath and sighed, looking as if he planned to go down the hole himself.

"So, what are you doing here?" John asked crossing his arms and leaning against the post next to the hole.

"Here to make sure you're still breathing." Turning his attention away from the hole. "Lilith normally doesn't play with her food."

John scratching at his jaw line. "How do you know Lilith?" This guy kept popping up in the strangest places.

"We go back a little bit." The officer shrugged with a smile.

"Alright, what are you?" John asked. The first time he smelled sweet chili, they'd been attacked by an angel. John's blue eyes narrowed. "I'm betting angel."

The officer raised a brow. "You pick up quick. Call me Zech."

Shovel in hand Lilith cut down the nemas. Shoving the metal end of the shovel into the mass, stomach acid and blood singeing her face and roasting the flesh off her hand.

The thicker tendrils were segmented like wriggling millipedes that slipped and splashed in the turbid water. Brown froth floated to the surface, the water rolling as the creature moved beneath.

"Must be murder time." Lilith pulled out her blade, the shovel in her other hand, plunging into the chaos in front of her.

The water now splashing at her chest, she struggled to keep the torch above the waterline, which glistened like a parking lot splattered in bright colorful oil slicks after rain.

The sludge in the bottom of the tank helped her secure her footing, an errant tentacle snaked around her leg. She slammed the shovel down, risking her only source of light.

More iridescent ooze floated to the top of the water. The smell of petrol and bile filled the space. She gagged and coughed as more of the creature floated through the water.

A hush fell in the tank, broken only by the occasional bubble rising to the surface, burping as it broke. Her torch sputtering, she only reached the halfway mark of the second tank. She surged forward to the back wall. Leaning against it, she gasped for air.

The wall shuddered, tendrils wrapped around her wrist and up her arm, attempting to consume her.

John stumbled back. He hit the white paneling of the house with a crunch. His right foot slipped into the basement window box, crushing the corpses of dead plants beneath his heels. His bare toes squelching in the decomposing matter.

"Woah, calm down there, buddy," Zech said. He held his hands up as if approaching a startled hodag, "I'm a friend."

A loud gurgling sound came from the tank.

"I bet you are about as 'friendly' as the other guy," John said. "Do you have flaming weapons of destruction as well?"

"You've met Gabe," Zech grinned and chuckled.

"Met? Met! He tried to kill me!" John pulled his foot out of the window box and shook off the muck. "Gabe wrecked my apartment and destroyed my bed." John checked the entrance of the septic tank. He hoped things were going better for Lilith. "I really liked that bed."

"No, not you," Zech said. He circled around the hole. "Lilith. He was trying to kill that monstrously beautiful woman."

"Are you here to kill her?" John asked looking around for the other shovel. *Weapon, I need a weapon.*

"You don't need a weapon," Zech said. "I'm not here to hurt you." He kicked a rock into the hole. It splattered as it hit the shallow water below.

"How do you keep doing that?" John spotted the second shovel that hid in the grass.

"What?" Zech picked up the shovel, tossing it to John.

John missed and the shovel clattered onto the concrete porch. "It's like you are reading my mind."

"Angel power," Zech wiggled his eyebrows. "I know the hearts of men."

John picked up the shovel and held it like a shield between him and Zech trying to defend his thoughts from invasion. "Great."

"Yep." Zech kicked another couple of loose rocks down into the opening of the tank, each thudding and splashing.

"Can you turn it off?" John asked. "Really don't like the idea of someone in my head."

"I have no idea." Zech took a seat on the back step that lead into Iris's kitchen. He looked John over as if sizing him up. "You could ask Lil. She seems to be pretty good at blocking me out."

"She probably doesn't even realize she can." John retook his post over the entrance of the tank. "She told me all the angels want her dead."

Zech flashed a grin. "Not all of us." He leaned back against the glass door causing the frame to squeak.

"Gabe has me convinced otherwise," John gripped the shovel.

Zech sat back up, leaning forward he replied, "I may be the only one."

"Then you're friends?" John stabbed the shovel into the ground.

"No." Zech crossed his arms and glared at John.

"Enemies?" John reached for the shovel.

"Not that either." Zech pursed his lips and balled his fists up.

John scratched at his chin and tried to ignore the cold seeping into his toes. "Does she even know you exist?"

Zech didn't respond. He exhaled sharply through his nose.

"Are you stalking her?" John asked.

"No." Zech shook his head. A rolling peal of thunder, like Sunday church bells rippled through the air. Zech went on, "I'm here to ask you a favor."

Encased in darkness, Lilith flailed and struggled against the monsters that held her. The occasional cracks of light came from the torch. She had no idea how it stayed lit.

The tendrils arched away from the light.

Lilith lashed out at anything that touched her. Black blood and blue bile broiled and crackled across her skin. The smell of burning flesh filled her nostrils. Her labored breaths mimicked the flickering torch.

The enclosed space ebbed and flowed from focus. *I need to find another fuel source.* She tumbled forward, head first into the water trying to squirm between the tentacles. She grasped for the torch. When she broke the surface—flaming shovel in hand—a murky film of nemas blood covered the concrete box. Her eyes burned. Clumps of goo had congealed on the surface.

She grabbed at a handful of the curdled mass. "Worth a shot," she said.

Another wave of nemas came over the wall into the second tank. Tentacles wrapped around her ankles and up her calves. She dumped the goo on the torch. A brilliant blue blaze filled the space. Lighting up Lilith's grotesque smile.

"You'd be doing yourself a favor. Lil has something the gal in charge wants. If she gets it, the lot of us take off." Zech stared at John, waiting for a reaction.

"Ask Lilith for it," John shook his naked foot, muck flinging onto the ground.

"I would if I could," he said a sad smile flashed across his face. "I'm only asking you to keep an eye out for it. Old wooden box may have a carving of two crossed sickles on the top."

"Does it really contain a skull?" John asked.

"Open it up and have a look. He won't bite," Zech said.

"And why can't you ask Lilith?" John watched the angel creep up to the entrance of the tank like a cat stalking prey in the grass.

"Let's say it has to do with the powers that be," Zech said.

"When you say the powers that be, do you mean," John pointed to the heavens.

"No, not that far up the chain," Zech said. "Will you get the box?"

"Why do you need it?" John rubbed his foot on his pant leg, trying to warm it up.

"Someone needs our help," Zech said. Icy droplets began to fall from the sky. They moved under the cover of the porch. The hail pinged and clattered on the roof, rolling down and into the yard.

"Cryptic," John said. "If I get the box, the kill happy angel goes away? Could you protect me from him?"

"If that's all you want," Zech rolled his shoulders back. "But you have to stay away from Lilith."

"Don't know if I can," John smiled. A world filled with unknown creatures and adventures? This was what he dreamed of as a child.

Zech frowned. "Where is Lilith anyway?"

"Fighting monsters," John pointed at the opening.

"Think about it," Zech said. "It can be helpful to have an angel around." He walked across the yard, back towards the fence line. "I'll check in with you later." Zech paused and turned around. "Be careful, John. She's dangerous."

John kept an eye on Zech as he walked away. "I half expected him to fly off," he said. "Can't wait to hear what Lilith has to say about him."

Lilith coughed. She could feel her eardrums collapsing. If she wasn't careful, the whole tank could go with the amount of explosive gastric juices it contained. She slid down a tendril, dropping into the third part of the tank with a splash. An opalescent nest rolled in front of her. Tentacles the size of gnarled tree trunks, shuddering and shaking at the exposed flame she held. Patches of her skin disappeared eaten away by the acid, while the skin on her face and arms stretched taut from burns. Her muscles and bones ached from use and abuse. She waved the flame through the air, trying to clear a path to the core of the mass.

"Woah, you got big." The woven bamboo-like ball at the back of the tank, was the goal. She rushed toward it.

Slice. The blade splitting the tendril in two. A wash of more fluids splattering across her.

Stab. Into the writhing mass before her.

Thud. As she impacted with the wall, a tentacle across her chest.

A waltz of death and destruction. Lilith worked her way through the tank.

She knew the movements well enough that she didn't have to think.

Swish. A tentacle flew overhead and Lilith ducked.

Swoop. Her arm knocked aside, flailing the air to balance before shattering on the tank wall.

Thwack. The blade of the shovel struck against the stagnant water.

Moving to an unheard melody. Until her unwilling partner looped a tendril around her foot, flipping her onto her back.

From beneath the creature, she hacked at what held her. Success marked by a fountain of ooze. Standing up and wiping the goo from her lower jaw, exposed her teeth and jawbone. Leaving a skeletal grin.

"I've had enough of you," she snarled. Her teeth clattered, the flesh of her cheek fluttering, dripping blue blood, onto bare white bone. She gathered more curdled gunk from the top of the stagnant water and added it to the torch. Blazing blue flames engulfed what remained of the shovel. She charged forward, flame first, to the overfed monstrosity. She made this mess and now she would clean it up.

The nemas encircled her in one last embrace.

Silence.

Followed by a brilliant shock wave of light and sound.

John never saw the ground ripple before.

Pops of blue flames flared out of the ground.

Cracks appeared in the grass, and a poplar tree fell with a crunch.

It grew quiet before parts of the yard sunk. Disappearing in chunks.

John put a bare foot forward, testing the ground with his big toe. It didn't sink beneath him so he moved toward the edge of the damage. A large hole filled with charred cement and the smell of smoke overwhelmed him.

"Lilith?" John called.

No answer.

He inched a little closer. "Lilith?" The ground betrayed him and gave way. Dropping him into the pit.

He landed on all fours with a thud. Ash billowed around him. The cement walls wore a thick black crust.

No liquid, no nemas.

Standing up, he wiped the ash from his hands on his jeans. Each step kicked up clouds of dust. A crack of white light cut across the floor where he fell in.

A gash from his wrist to his elbow started throbbing. His foot knocked a blackened form, that grinned up at him.

"Lilith?" He hoped she could come back from this. It wouldn't surprise him if it belonged to someone else she'd stuck in her sewer.

Picking up the skull and pushing around the dirt, he checked for other bones.

His arm dribbled blood onto the skull. "Sorry about that," John said, and with the other sleeve, he tried to wipe the blood off. Instead he smeared it across the forehead, the blood and ash mixing together. "Well let's get you out of here," John threw the skull up out of the hole. It crunched on the grass as it landed.

"Now, how do I get out?" he asked. A thin stream of blood dripped on the floor of the tank.

The swirling ash settled, and then began to vibrate on the floor. Grass and dirt rained down on him as it worsened. Pulsating as if alive, the ash pulled and pushed around the underground space.

A tibia smacked him in the ankle and darted towards the sky. A femur flew past, cutting him on the cheek. He ducked as vertebrae rose from the floor, lining up and shooting out of the tank in rapid succession as if fired from a cannon.

A second femur formed in front of him. Reaching out, he grabbed onto it. The bone jerked him up, grating him across the cement wall and back out into the yard. He let go once he could feel the dry grass beneath him.

On the ground, a skeleton started to form, joints popping and reconnecting. Sinews stitching and lacing to muscles.

"Oh boy," John said. "Definitely Lilith." His face pulsed and chest burned looking down the sweater he'd ripped open the exposed skin which looked a bit like raw hamburger. "Yummy." Testing it with his finger, the flesh wept in response. "Ow."

A hissing and grinding came from the skeleton. Struggling, it stood up. Muscles forming on the legs. Through the ribcage, lungs expanded and contracted as it hobbled towards him. Internal organs disappeared behind a wall of muscle.

John blinked and blinked again. Out of sheer horror he wanted to be nowhere near that thing. A string of expletives flew from his mouth. Running across the yard to the house, he disappeared down the stairs.

18

TOIL AND TROUBLE

Lilith shuddered. New bones and skin always felt itchy, like she needed to stretch everything out. She saw John run back into the house. She knew it's one thing to see someone awaken from the dead, but quite another thing entirely to watch them build back up from scratch.

She walked down the stairs, cool concrete underneath the bare souls of her feet. Opening the front door, which swished across the blue carpet as she walked inside. Down the hall, the bathroom door slammed closed.

"John?" Lilith tried the bathroom door. The knob rattled, but wouldn't open. "Are you okay?"

"No!" he yelled. "Are you going to eat me?"

"No," she said. "I'm fine. I do this all the time. I told you I cannot die." She ran her fingers through fresh hair.

"Do you have skin yet? Or you still all fleshy?"

"You saw me regenerate from scratch?" she asked.

"Yes!" he exclaimed. "I fell in the tank and found your skull. Sorry, I spilled some blood on it. But I wiped it off and then bones, sinew, organs starting appearing. Out of nowhere."

Lilith bit her lip. This was bad, really bad. "I can smell the blood through the door," she said. "When you're ready come out and I'll have something mixed up for that."

She ran to the kitchen, throwing open cupboard doors and pulling out an array of items.

Her skin tingled, muscles contracting at random beneath it. She jumped when she saw Connor standing there with his arms folded across his chest.

"I nearly lost some of my folk today," he said.

"I don't have time for this," she said. "Pass me the kava root."

"You'll make time," he said. Connor pushed a bag of powder out of the cupboard and onto the counter. It fell with a slight poof.

"I don't have time to deal with a temper tantrum, Connor," Lilith said.

"Oh?" he motioned down the hall. "Am I getting in the way of you playing with your new toy? Leave the boy alone. I like him."

"He's not a toy," she said. "John is my friend." She frowned as she pulled out a mortar and pestle from beneath the counter. The words rocked her. They even silenced Connor for a few beats.

"What are you mixing up?" Connor watched as Lilith mashed a variety of roots and spices in the mortar and spitting in it and giving another couple of quick stirs.

"I started from scratch. You can't smell it," she said. "But his blood is driving me crazy."

"His blood?" he asked.

"Yes," Lilith massaged her temples, rubbing the skin on her face.

"Poor bastard," Connor said. "You could eat him, you know. No need to add extra suffering."

"He has dragon blood," she said. She turned on the sink. Relieved as water swished out of the tap. She added it to the mix.

"Let him be, or kill him and eat him, then find someone else." Connor said. "Friends do not turn friends into dragons."

"No, if he's going to die, I might as well make use of him," She said. "Not a word from you or any of the clan."

"Contract wouldn't let me anyway," Connor watched as she

poured the concoction into a cup. Lilith heard the bathroom door open. Footsteps coming down the hall.

"You know you're naked, right?" John asked from the hall.

"Yes, again." she said. "Astute observation."

"Whatever you're doing could probably wait till you get dressed," John shuffled at the entrance to the kitchen.

"Not if I want you to stop bleeding on my walls," Lilith turned around and thrust the cup towards him.

"What is it, anyway?" John took the cup, rocking it back and forth, causing the muddy brown concoction to swirl.

"Something that'll fix you up," Lilith said.

Connor rolled his eyes as he stood leaning against the cupboard door.

"What's in it?" John asked.

"Nothing you can't find in nature," Lilith looked back to where John took refuge in the hall.

"Arsenic occurs in nature." John slid down the wall, sitting on the matted carpet.

"What was that?" she asked. Turning around, she folded her arms across her bare chest.

"Uh," John said. "What happened to the scars on your hands?"

"When I die, I go right back to the beginning," she sighed. "I told you this. No scars, no tattoos. Didn't you believe me?"

"Seeing is believing, I guess," John said. "This smells awful."

"Tastes worse," Lilith leaned a hip on the counter. "Won't get any better if you wait."

"Well as long as you didn't spit in it," John took a swig and began coughing.

"Drink it all," Lilith went back to the counter, putting everything away.

Connor had disappeared.

"Tastes like mud." John crossed his arms over his chest as if trying to hide his skin.

"I'll see if I can find you a shirt." Lilith didn't mind being naked. She walked into the room across the hall and ruffled through a pile of unused clothes on her floor. She found a t-shirt that might fit him. When she came out, John lay passed out in the hall.

She put it down next to him.

Lilith retrieved her journal and made a note that she gave the brew to John. She couldn't remember anything that happened in the tank. Except now she hungered for John's blood.

She checked the bathroom. Demolished but easy enough to fix.

Lilith stood over John again, her feelings strangely filled with regret and sorrow. He was going to wake up with a splitting headache.

She went back into her room and shut the door.

Stumbling in the dark she tripped over another pile of clothes, and swore at it. She would need to have a word with the clan about where they left things, though she couldn't bring herself to care at the moment. She grabbed at things to cover her skin. It didn't matter what, as long as she put something on. A strange tightness filled her eyes, one she hadn't felt that she recalled. The seams of the thick denim scratched her legs, the shirt felt tight and loose at the same time, in different locations. *This sucks.*

She returned to her friend, her steps heavier and slower than before. John snored in the hall outside the bedroom door. She leaned against the hallway wall, sliding down and sitting on the carpet. *Being my friend is never a good idea.* Lilith thumped the back of her head against the plaster.

Keeping people away keeps them safe. Tears slid down her cheeks. She dashed them away with the back of her hand. Lilith waited for John to wake up.

"Ow," John muttered.

Lilith stood up and went to his side. "About time," Lilith said. "Sure, took your time healing."

"Healing?" John asked.

Lilith surveyed where the damage had been, no blood, no scabs. The potion had taken hold.

John grabbed the shirt from the floor, tearing off the tattered sweater and pulling it on. "Thanks."

"Don't mention it," Lilith said. "Come on. I'm hungry."

Walking out of the house, she followed the smells of fried food down the road.

"I sure do a lot of walking with you around," John grumbled, rubbing his eyes.

"Do you have to drive everywhere?" Lilith asked, marching ahead.

John kept pace beside her.

She glanced back, in his neck, a vein throbbed. She looked away, digging her fingernails into her palms, distracting herself from the voice in her mind that reminded her of how satisfying it would be to rip open his throat and feast.

"Walking makes sense in a city," John said. "Here, everything is all spread out." They reached the parking lot of the plasma center. "Come on. Let's take my car."

"Fine," Lilith said.

The two of them got in the vehicle and John started the car. A low purr came from the idling engine.

An olive-green escort pulled up in front of the center. Mike and Lisa sat in the front seat. Mark toddled out the building door and climbed in the back seat.

"Mike was supposed to be on shift tonight," John said.

The back of Lilith's neck tingled when she looked at Lisa. The girl had that bit of her blood. "We should follow them," she said. Her stomach growled, and she rubbed at the tingling spot.

"No," John turned his head away.

"Why not?" Lilith asked. "Has Mark said anything about what happened with the hodags?"

"No," John said.

"You don't forget something like that." Lilith said. "I think the girl has something that belongs to me."

John pulled out of the parking lot following, after them despite his declaration that he wouldn't. The green car darted through the lanes of traffic, like a minnow trying to escape a larger fish.

"Do they know they're being followed?" Lilith watched as Mike weaved in between the lanes without indicating.

"Mike can't drive," John growled. Either he was hurting still or just in a bad mood.

"You're one to talk," Lilith dug her nails into her seat. They lurched around a corner and into a parking spot at the local steakhouse, the front of the car facing away from the restaurant. John put the car into park and cracked the back windows.

Lilith sniffed at the air, "Something smells delicious."

"Probably the meat." He said watching Mike, walk in through the rearview mirror.

Lilith's hand was on the door handle. "Now what?"

"We wait."

"Argh, you've got to be kidding me!" She snarled, pulling her hand away from the handle like it bit her. "Why wait?" She wriggled in her seat, the denim scraping against the car upholstery. "Let's go in."

"No."

"Why not?" Lilith pulled a booted foot up onto the car seat. Ringing through the parking lot came the upbeat sound of country music. The speakers on the restaurant were sirens for a good time, decent drinks, and cheap steak.

"Lisa and Mark are still in the car," John said. He pulled his phone out, looking at the screen and then put it in the cup holder.

Lilith rifled through the wrappers like unfiled documents carefully selecting pieces of the waxed paper, ripping them into strips and consuming them as they waited. It was like watching a shredder make documents disappear, one strip at a time.

"What are you doing?" John asked gripping the steering wheel.

"Cleaning," she said, coughing through a mouthful of yellow wrapper. "And I'm hungry." Crumpling up another wrapper, she smacked her lips on the mouthful of wet wax paper. Lilith continued until all the fast food trash was gone. "We could be all sneaky," Lilith said. She turned in her seat peeking out from the gap between the headrest and the seat, staring out the rear windshield at the restaurant. "He'd never know we were there."

John's hand searched the side of his chair and pushed a small lever. It whirred as his chair reclined. "He went in by himself. He's probably picking up food."

"True, but I could get some scraps," Lilith licked her lips, imaging the juices of red meat dripping down her throat.

John pulled his phone out from the cup holder handing it to Lilith. "Here."

Swiveling around and facing forward, she gazed at the phone in her hand. "What am I going to do with this?"

Shrugging his shoulders. "Play a game. Surf the web."

Swiping at the screen with a gloved finger, replied, "I can't."

Lilith and modern tech didn't seem to get along. Automatic doors, touch screens, and digital cameras didn't acknowledge her existence.

John bolted up and looked over at his device. "What do you mean, you can't? Is something wrong with my phone?"

She tapped the screen again. "The screen doesn't register my finger." Lilith handed the phone back with a sigh.

John shifted in his seat, "You ok?"

"I'm fine," Lilith said. She huffed and looked out the window, a sea of trucks blocked her view of the road. Turning around in her seat again she stared at the building willing Mike to come out.

John arched his back trying to stretch it out. A muffled pop rewarded his efforts. "Can you use touch screens?"

"No," Lilith said.

"I'm sure there are lots of people that can't operate a smartphone."

"Yeah, right," she said.

"I could get you a stylus."

"What is that?" Lilith asked.

John held an invisible pencil in his hand and drew in the air. "It's a little stick that you use to operate the screen."

Lilith snorted. "And when I lose it, or it breaks?" Turning around a third time, pulling her legs up on the seat, and leaning her back against the dashboard.

John released his seatbelt with a click. "Right."

"Man, I'm hungry," she said.

"We could go get food," John checked his phone. "I don't think Mike, Mark, and Lisa are up to anything. Or you could eat some more wrappers?"

Lilith glared at him. "I ate them all," The wrappers no longer crinkled under Lilith's feet. She enjoyed the quiet, till John's phone chirped.

He stared at the screen. "Better offer?"

"What offer?" Lilith asked. "Maybe you're right. Let's go get food. This waiting is killing me." Her stomach growled.

"Lisa just messaged me," John said. "Saying she can't do dinner because she got a better offer."

"Mike and Mark are a better offer?" Lilith asked. "Wow, you are really failing at the whole relationship thing."

"I'm not interested in Lisa." John rested his head on the steering wheel.

Lilith rolled her eyes. "Right, your heart belongs to Sarah," she put her hands by her face and batted her eyes. "By the way, have you heard anything from her?"

"No," John said. "She hasn't returned any of my messages or calls."

Something niggled at the back of Lilith's mind. How did Lisa get her blood? She thought Sarah had eaten it. "How long is he going to take in there?" Lilith asked. She resorted to playing with the headrest. Pulling it forward listening to it click, then letting it go, snapping back to its original place.

"Depends on when the order was placed. Fifteen, maybe even thirty minutes."

"Seriously?" She turned around and slammed her head back on the headrest. "It's meat. It should not take so long."

John rubbed his hands across his face. "You know they cook it, right?"

"What a waste of perfectly good meat," Lilith said. "This is why I'm not a fan of civilized society. How long has it been?"

Looking at the clock he replied, "About ten minutes."

"I'm going to go mad." She reclined her seat back. It clicked like a child's pull-along toy.

John rolled his eyes. "This is more or less a stakeout. They are long and boring and sometimes lead to nothing."

Lilith's seat clicked up slowly. "There has been no steak."

"It's a phrase," he said. "You could sleep."

"I'm not tired," Lilith's words came out like a toddler whining and refusing to take a nap.

"How about a game?" John looked up at the roof of the car.

"Like what?" Lilith took both her hands and scratched at the base of her scalp.

"I-spy?" John offered.

"You have to be kidding me," Lilith dropped her hands into her lap. "I still think we should go in."

"I'll go first," John said. "I spy with my little eye, something beginning with M."

"Mike."

"No," John said gripping the steering wheel. It squeaked in his grip. "That's not how the game works."

Lilith grabbed his face with one hand and turned it to look out the back of the car at the restaurant. "Mike is coming out of the building."

A muffled, "Oh," came out of his pursed lips.

Mike carried a couple of large white plastic bags on his arms. He kicked at the door of his car and Mark opened it grabbing the food.

"That's a lot of steak." Lilith said smacking her lips. Lilith fought with her curiosity over Lisa and the blood, and the hunger that gnawed away at her gut. "Think they'll eat it all?"

"Let's find out," John said. "Better offer," he muttered as he started the car and followed them out of the parking lot.

They shot down Main Street. Buildings that were once houses now claimed and altered into business, most of them closed for night. A bronze cowboy, riding a bucking stallion lit up with the passing headlights sat in the middle of a roundabout. It looked as if it was going to take off down the road heading for the rodeo grounds.

"Come on," Lilith said, fidgeting in her seat. "You don't want to lose them, do you?"

The engine revved as the vehicle lurched through a yellow light. "If I go to quickly, they'll notice me."

Sitting back in her seat she replied, "Snooping is not for me."

The indicator clicked as John switched lanes. "No kidding."

The car took a sharp right and went down a gravel road, stopping outside of a white shed.

Lilith looked down the lane covered in tall trees. "What is that place?"

John parked on the shoulder of the road. "Do you want them to see us?"

"No," Lilith hopped out of the car, her boots crunching on the gravel as she headed down the road.

"Hold on." John leaned across the middle, grabbing her by the arm. "We have no idea if this is their final stop."

Lights flickered on in the shed, the hum of a generator filling the cold empty night. "I think they'll be sticking around," Lilith shook him off and continued down the lane.

Big billows of John's breath filled the air like smoke coming from a dragon's snout. It drifted up and disappeared in the light of the moon.

Lilith could hear murmurs of Lisa, Mike, and Mark's conversation inside.

"This is it." Lilith moved closer to the shed door covered in flaky white paint.

A small puff of smoke escaped through a crack.

John's nose wrinkled at the smell. "Ugh," he coughed, "This was the better offer? Smells like a skunk died."

"Yeah, a skunk," Lilith said. She started to chuckle. "I'm sure that's what you're smelling." A heavy off-beat bass line started to thump out from the shed. Lilith walked towards the door, as if being summoned to appear.

"What are you doing?" John slid himself between her and the shed.

"I'm going to go talk to them," She tried to side step around him.

"No." John shook his head. "Let's make sure we know what they're doing first." He motioned her around to the side of the shed where a large crack let light out from a split panel. John and Lilith peered in the crack of the knotted wood wall. The bass beat caused the boards to tremble under Lilith's fingers.

"Man, are you sure they said tonight?" Mark asked, a spurt of coughing followed the question. A wisp of smoke snuck out through the crack.

"Yep," Mike said. "Should show up around 8 or 9."

"Next time," Mark said. "Nail down a time, would ya?"

"Why? You got anything better to do?" Mike asked.

"No," Mark replied. "Except keep you from smoking all the product."

A barking laugh came out of the shed. There was some shuffling and it sounded like one of the two had moved away from the conversation.

"Sounds like fun in there." Lilith said. "I'm going in."

"You can't." John pulled her back down, his shoes scraping across the cold gravel. "We should get going."

"They're expecting someone," Lilith said. "I don't see why it can't be me."

"Maybe because they probably know who they're expecting."

"I'll be fine," Lilith brushed her hands off on her dark jeans. "I want to have some fun, anyway."

"No." John scrambled after her, his feet kicking up gravel that clicked against the shed wall as he crawled around the corner.

"What are they going to do?" Lilith asked, opening the door. The light of the shed flooding half her face the other half still hidden in a dark shadow. "Kill me?"

"Lilith," John said through gritted teeth.

She slammed the door on him.

19

TENJONAME

L ilith smiled. The shed smelled of dirt and growth. Above her, bare wooden trusses and beneath her boots, a packed dirt floor. A pile of old wooden orchard boxes were stacked near the entrance on the left. A shabby couch and a worse-for-wear recliner in the middle of the shed were positioned like a makeshift living room. Shag carpet, a patchwork of faded blue, brown, and orange made up a rug. Some of the orchard boxes had been turned into a coffee table. White carryout containers were strewn across the table casting scents of fat and meat through the space.

Sheets on a clothesline portioned off the back of the shed. *This place is perfect for a prank.* She thought, clicking her jaw. She turned and grabbed a piece of timber that leaned on the wall and slid it into the iron handles on the backside of the door.

"Evening boys," she said. No sign of Lisa. Perhaps she was behind the curtain.

"Who the hell are you?" Mike asked, turning off the speaker.

Mark set up defenses behind the shabby gray couch. Lilith could smell the sweat rolling off him, repugnant and filled with panic.

She turned her attention to Mark. "You don't remember me?"

"No," Mark said. His breathing had become erratic. And was that sweet chili pepper she smelled? Angels could mess with memory. Maybe that's why he couldn't remember the hodags and the mess at the center.

"We've met before, but you might have been a little distracted," Lilith pumped her eyebrows at him.

Mark grimaced as if trying not to remember. "I thought I was high."

"You probably were," Lilith said.

"Mark, what is she talking about?" Mike asked.

"I can't remember," Mark's eyes seemed to cloud over a little bit.

"Best to keep it that way. Are you going to eat that?" she asked pointing at the open Styrofoam container on the table.

She didn't wait for an answer. Pulling off her gloves, she tucked them into her back pocket. The Styrofoam squeaked in her hand as she picked up one of the half-eaten meals. She scooped out sweet corn flavored with lemon pepper and butter with her fingers, shoveling it into her mouth. She moved on to the remainder of the mashed potatoes using two fingers as a spoon. She savored the salty mush sliding down her throat.

"What are you doing?" Mike asked.

"Eating." Lilith ripped a chunk out of half a sirloin steak, chewing on the savory meat. Lilith held the Styrofoam take-out box up to her mouth, draining the remaining liquid. Fatty, salty, and sweet juices dribbled on her chin.

Wiping them off, she licked the back of her hand then began to break pieces off the container, devouring it as well. It didn't taste like much, but the container was gone before long.

Mike took a couple of steps towards her, then shook his head as if he had seen a magic trick he couldn't quite figure out.

"How much pot is behind the curtain?" Lilith asked, licking her fingers. She sniffed the air, a mix of skunk and citrus filled her nose.

"Nothing is behind the curtain," Mark came out from behind the couch and stood in front of the partition.

"Uh huh." Like a magician moving onto her next trick, she pulled the curtain down revealing rows of dark green plants.

Seedlings were on the front tables, followed by juveniles, and then adult plants in the back. All were basking in grow lights and quiet humming heaters. Lisa came out from the last row, wearing gloves with a pair of garden shears in her hand.

"That's a whole lot of nothing," Lilith said, walking back towards the adult plants and pulling in a deep breath. "I can see why the little one is so jumpy." Mark and Mike stayed back by the couch.

"Hello Lilith," Lisa put the shears down on the table. "You turn up in all sorts of unusual places, don't you?"

"I can say the same for you," Lilith eyed Lisa's pendant. Old magic pulsed from the carving powered by a sweet smell Lilith knew, her blood. "You have something that belongs to me. How did you get my blood?"

Anger flashed through Lisa's dark eyes. Then she smiled. "Blood shouldn't be blue."

"Yeah," Lilith rubbed her knuckles on her shirt. "But I'm full of the stuff."

"Good to know." Lisa dumped a handful of clippings into a plastic bag.

"I'm going to need that charm for a moment," Lilith said.

"No," Lisa's tone flattened, no room for negotiation.

"I'll give it back." Lilith moved in, grabbing the charm and sticking it in her own mouth. She could taste what remained of her blood, old and clotted with a bit of rubbing alcohol. The irksome feeling from the night of the hodag attack disappeared. Then a cocktail of flavors hit her, a variety of blood, both animal and human. The charm itself tasted of sulfur and rotten apples- dragon bone. Lilith spit it out.

"Who do you think you are?" Lisa used her shirt to wipe Lilith's spit off the necklace. Her serene smile gone, her lips pulled to a tight line.

"No one." A wide smile cracked her face. "How long have you been dead?"

Lisa blinked once and blinked again. "I don't even know where to begin with that question."

Lilith thought of how she used dragon skin. For her, flesh and blood were no problem. She avoided the bones, too much power, too risky, and always hungry. "The charm has been keeping you alive," Lilith said. "You've been stealing lives."

"You need to leave," Lisa wrapped her fingers around the pruning shears.

"Don't worry," Lilith said. "I was never here." She walked over to Mark and Mike who hadn't moved from behind the dilapidated couch.

Mike's brow furrowed. "What?"

"You annoy me." Lilith cocked her head and turned her attention to Mark. She leaned in a little closer, sniffing near his neck. "You smell kind of good."

Mark cowered, covering his neck, and shuffled closer to Mike.

Lilith started for the door.

"Lisa, one last thing," she said. "Keep away from John, he doesn't need to deal with your kind of crazy." Lilith pulled at the timber, it squealed against the metal.

"No," Lisa came forward, she crossed her arms. "I won't be doing that. You think you could stop me?"

Show time. Lilith pushed her makeshift lock back into place. She squished her fingers into the flesh in front of her ears, placing her fingers in her mouth. Grunting, she made a sickening pop, then turned around, letting her jaw waggle like a turkey's wattle.

Her breath now came out as a raspy gurgle. Mucus and drool dripped on the floor. She wrapped her fingers around her tongue. Tugging it forward, she cleared her airway. Then let it swing back and forth. It felt good to have everything pulled apart.

Mike's eyes widened and Mark paled at the sight.

Lisa hadn't moved.

No screams? Fine then. She covered her eyes and dug her thumbs into the sockets. Her eyeballs squelched, popping out and dangling by a nerve. Her fingers now free, she held her globes up, looking at Mike and Mark.

They let out terrified yelps. When she turned her sights on Lisa, she hadn't moved. Nor did she appear frightened or amused.

The shed door shaking behind, her made everyone in the room jump. John must be trying to get in. She let go of her eyes. Using her free hand, she popped the one eye in and then the other. A few quick blinks and her vision cleared. She let her tongue flop about as she lined her jaw back up with a crack, she pushed it back in place. Throwing her head back like a seagull she gulped until her tongue fell back in place.

She took one last glance back. Mike and Mark cowered behind the couch. Lisa seemed unfazed by the whole event.

Lilith made a mental note, that girl would be a problem.

Lilith slid the timber out of the door, letting it fall with a thud on the ground. She opened the door, walking out into the dark. The door slammed shut behind her.

John came barreling towards her. She grabbed him by the shoulders, swinging him around, stones skittering from beneath their feet as they came to a stop. "What are you doing?" she asked.

"Trying to break down the door," John huffed. "The shed was silent, then someone inside started screaming. He crossed his arms over his chest. "What happened in there?"

"Mark and Mike are easily startled. That's all." She walked up the road, back towards the car.

"What did you do?" John asked again.

"Nothing," Lilith scrunched her eyes, helping them to settle back into place.

"Right," John said. "Your nothing always seems to be something really painful."

Lilith rubbed her jaw, the bones clicking as she shifted it back and forth.

"Are you okay?" John asked. "Mike and Mark didn't try to attack you, did they?"

Lilith laughed. "No. I'm fine. My jaw just pops out occasionally."

"That sucks," John said. "Did you find out why Mike has been missing so much work?"

"He has a side project he's been working on with Mark and Lisa," Lilith said. "Has Lisa always been so, intense?"

EDEN'S OUTCAST

"That's one way of putting it," John said. "Sarah told me that in her room, she has this massive board with the next five years planned out. She has a party every time she checks a goal off."

Lilith nodded. "Be careful around that one. I'd hate to see you end up on her white board."

"I don't think I'm here type." John laughed as they got in his car. "How is it that no one notices all the supernatural creatures running around?"

"Did you ever think to go looking for a hodag or a fairy before you met me?" Lilith fastened her seatbelt.

"No, those were stories before I met you," he said. "But I'm glad I know about it now." John turned the keys in the ignition the car sputtering to life.

"Be careful," Lilith said. "People that do go looking, tend to go missing."

"No one notices?" John asked. "I mean strange bite marks and melting flesh should draw attention. Don't people ask questions?" He pulled out onto the road.

"People will rationalize these things, all the deaths can be broken down to something that occurs naturally," she said. "All things considered, you should be dead."

"I'm not going anywhere, Lilith," John gave her a smile. "I'm having too much fun."

Something twinged at the back of Lilith's mind. Guilt? Maybe. *Ugh, feelings,* she thought. Perhaps not the end of the world that John would be gone soon. She'd be able to replenish her dwindling stocks of dragon's blood and leather. *It'll be easier to kill a dragon, than to eat John.*

"Did you want to crash at my place tonight?" John asked. "Since your house doesn't currently have a working toilet. Or shower for that matter."

"Yeah, that would be great," Lilith said. "Are you hungry? I'm hungry."

"You're always hungry," John said, as they headed back to his place.

20

SPOT

John had spent the night going back and forth to the bathroom. He stared at the porcelain bowl and retched again. His gut trembled, muscles convulsing, chills spreading out from his gut. He pushed the handled flushing the toilet.

"John!" Lilith yelled from the other side of the closed door. "Food!"

John groaned. "Don't you ever think of anything else?" he asked.

"Sometimes," Lilith said. "Are you ok?"

"No," he said. Stumbling out of the bathroom. "I'm not feeling so hot."

"Let's get some food in you," Lilith said. "Do you have work today?"

"Yeah," he said. "Swing shift." He picked his computer chair up off the ground. One of the few pieces of furniture that had survived. John pressed his hands to the side of his head as he lowered himself into the chair. Out of habit he pressed the power button on his computer, it didn't turn on. None of the appliances in the apartment worked. Last night they had cleaned up the broken glass. The mattress and bed frame had been obliterated.

John had to use his shoulder to open the front door but at least he could close and lock it. He would not be getting his security deposit back.

"Maybe, you shouldn't go in to work," she said. "We'd have more time for food." Lilith stood by the door.

"We'd have to go out," John said. "Where do you want to eat?"

"Go?" she asked. "Give me a minute I'll run out and grab a couple of puppies. We can eat here."

"Puppies?" he asked.

"Baby dogs," she said. She raised a brow. "There was a whole box of them outside the store yesterday."

"You eat puppies," John said. "Of course you do." He rubbed his hands over his face.

Lilith shrugged her shoulders, "Easy food source."

"No," John said. Nausea rolled up from his gut. "We will not be eating puppies today."

"Would you rather have cat?" Lilith asked. "They tend to be a little bit harder to catch."

John's mouth was agape. He closed it. "How about anything I'd consider a pet is off the menu."

"Puppy tends to get caught in my teeth anyway," Lilith tapped her chin. "Dumpster behind the

McDonald's might work," Lilith said. She cocked her head to the side. "Or Wendy's."

John headed for the bathroom, again. He didn't have a chance to close the door. But there was nothing left to expel from his stomach.

"What?" Lilith asked. "Was it something I said?"

"That's disgusting," he said. John turned on the bathroom sink letting the water run. He rinsed out his mouth and then gulped down a couple of cold handfuls. He splashed his face using the towel to dry it.

"Food is food," Lilith said. She tapped her foot on the ground. "It can't kill me. Also I can eat in bulk without having to pay for it."

"You know for someone that has been around since the beginning of time you sure are cheap." John came out of the bathroom. "Why is that?"

"I have trouble holding on to money," she said. "With the exception of my journals. I tend to lose things."

"You're broke?" he asked. "How is that possible?" John pulled on his socks and shoes.

"As far as mankind is concerned, I don't exist," Lilith said. "Not like I can open a bank account. I remember a time before money and trade." Lilith leaned in the door frame.

John stared at the floor a long thin crack traveled like a road through his floor. *Definitely not getting my deposit back.*

"It can be hard to keep hold of things." She peeled at some of the loose paint on the door frame letting it flutter to the ground.

"You have your house," John said. Standing up grabbing his keys and heading out the door.

They walked down the stairs together. "When I do try to stash something away an archaeologist digs it's up and it's the find of the century," Lilith said. She threw her arms in the air. "Than my favorite necklace ends up on display at The National Museum! Stupid Pyramids."

John's stomach flipped like someone turning over a timer. He'd gone from nauseous to starving.

"I need to eat," he said. "I'm choosing where."

"If you're choosing then you're paying," Lilith said.

"I figured," John said. His car keys jangled in his hand. "Let's go somewhere with meat." He licked his lips at the thought of something red, raw, and wriggling. *I've been spending too much time with Lilith.* He push the key fob and the door unlocked with a click.

Lilith opened the door and paused. "Why don't you go and get food and meet back at my place," she said. "I really should check on the clan."

"Seriously?" John asked. Seemed odd that Lilith would delay getting food.

Lilith looked over her shoulder, her eyes narrowed. "Yeah."

John rolled his eyes. "Alright, I'll see you soon."

"Bye." Lilith slammed the door walking away from the car.

The key clicked in the ignition and John took off to the nearest fast food drive thru he could find. He ordered a ungodly amount of burgers, and resisted the urge to eat them all. His gut hurt from hunger. He headed back to Lilith's place parking in the driveway.

John got out of the car bag of burgers in hand. He shifted his shoulders his shirt felt too tight, the collar scratched at his neck. He pulled at it with his free hand. The stitching in the cotton ripping loose. He felt strangled, he clawed at the shirt freeing himself from the tattered remains. He held the pieces in his hands, topless again. *Somehow this is Lilith's fault.*

A twinge in John's neck cascaded down his spine—crackling as it went—before stopping with a sharp stab in his tail bone, causing him to grunt. The muscles in his neck spasmed and he felt as if they were being shredded with a fork. He rolled his head back, clenching his teeth and suppressing a scream as the feeling rolled down his shoulders and into his arms. He panted, trying to catch his breath. "What the hell is happening?"

Something scuttled beneath the evergreen hedges.

"Just a robin," John said. His fest clenched on the paper bag, his fingers puncturing the paper.

His joints ached and the memory of the pain lingered in his muscles.

Loose rocks skittered and a flash of emerald disappeared beneath his car. His nostrils flared as he breathed out. John knelt down with a grunt, gravel pressing into his palm. He held the burgers up to keep them off the ground. Nothing. *Just because supernatural creatures exist doesn't mean they'll be everywhere you go.* He closed his eyes and exhaled. When he opened them a set of yellow eyes were staring at him from the front wheel well. A hodag darted out and grabbed the bag ripping it out of John's grasp. Scampering towards the backyard.

John threw his head back and let a roar come out from deep within his gut. "Drop it!"

The little monster dropped the bag with a yelp. Shoulders shaking, it turned around and faced John. It started to hack like a cat trying to let loose a hairball. A ball of phlegm came out landing on the ground.

John blinked and took a few steps closer. In the slime what looked like a finger bone glistened. "I wonder who that came from?" John asked. He picked up the bag of burgers, ripping away the top of the bag with the hodag phlegm dropping it to the ground. Sharp pain extended up his shins, ankles cold, the hem of his pants now came up to his calf. John needed to get inside. *Lilith will know what to do.*

The hodag flipped on its back exposing its belly, wriggling in the gray dust. It got up ,wagging its hindquarters as if it wanted to play. Three light green scales spotted its back side. Spiked tail swishing through the air.

John frowned. The last time he had been anywhere near one of these monstrosities it had try to eat him. His head throbbed, rubbing at his forehead he clenched his eyes closed. He needed to get into the house but the little monster blocked his way. John looked down at the bag of hamburgers in his hand. "These are suppose to be for me, you know." He sighed and pulled a wrapped burger out, chucking it into the backyard. The hodag gave chase, demolishing the burger. Bits of wrapper flew through the air as it ate.

John dashed to the top of the stairs. The hodag darted back across the lawn circling around his legs and then plopping down at the top of the stairwell as if guarding the entrance. He panted long pink tongue hanging out of its mouth over glistening white fangs.

"Where is the rest of your pack?" John asked. Scanning the quiet yard. The little guy seemed to be all alone. John groaned and buckled over, grabbing his stomach. His fingers stretched over his expanding gut. Releasing gas brought him some relief, but the smell of rotten eggs and pancakes engulfed him. He winced, his eyes stinging. It was as if someone had flicked the lights on in a darkened room without warning.

The hodag whimpered and shuddered coming down the steps. John froze as it nuzzled his leg. "You are downright friendly," John said. He leaned down and slowly reached out his hand and scratched behind his ears. The green scales felt like fingernails and clicked as he moved his hand over them. The hodag let out a happy chirp. Maybe the supernatural critters weren't so bad.

"Thing is, if I give you a name I'll get attached," John said. He had warmed up to the little fellow. He'd been distracting him from whatever had been going on in his gut. "Think I'll call you Cerebus." John kept going down the stairs to Lilith's door. His ankles felt like they were cracking fire raging through his bones. He braced himself against the door. Cerebus danced around his feet. "Besides I've always wanted a pet that could kill me."

Yanking the door open he went inside, Cerebus trotted in behind him. John's throat was on fire. He fell to the ground his hands clawing at the carpet as he crawled down the hall towards the kitchen.

"Lad is that you?" Connor asked. His voice had come out of the vent above the stove.

"Yeah," John said. He sat up against the kitchen cupboard hacking and coughing. "Not feeling the best." Cerebus plopped down beside him.

"I can see that," Connor said. He had come out of hiding and was standing on the counter above John.

"I must have ate something rotten, or maybe its a allergic reaction to something," John said. His shoulders shuddered and his fingers twitched. He grabbed his knees pulling them up to his chest.

"Allergies are one way of looking at it," Connor said. "Then again The Hag has always had a way of twisting trust."

"Out with it," John said. "What did she do now?" John arched his back trying to stretch out the ache.

"She spit in your drink," Connor said.

"Why would she do that?" John asked. His back spasmed like he had thrown a disc out. He let out a yelp.

Connor stepped back. "Oh, I'd tell you if I could. But I can't."

"Does this have to do with the contract?" John asked.

"Can't say," Connor said. He folded his arms across his chest.

"But you would if you could?" John asked.

Connor double pumped his two bushy red eyebrows in reply.

John's skin tingled and burned. He raked his hand across his arm, dead skin built up under his fingers as he scratched. His shoulders felt stretched, rubbing them against the kitchen cupboard help relieve the pain. "Worse than athlete's foot," John grimaced. The skin on his arm looked like cracked paint. He pinched at a piece of it with his fingers, peeling it away. Revealing thick translucent scales. He tapped on one of the oval shapes which was solid like a fingernail. The other soft scales shifted around it. Cerebus had moved away from him hiding by the side of the stove.

"Do you know what these are?" John asked.

Connor had darted to the top of the fridge legs dangling over the edge of the door. "Yep," Connor said. "Scales."

"No," John said. "I can't have scales." He shook his head.

"Dragon blood in your clan," Connor said. "You'd think someone in your family would have mentioned it. You've got all the marks about you." He started to list them off on his fingers. "Blue eyes, skin problems, and you smell a bit off."

"I do not smell," John said. A scream ripped out of him. He tried to stand but fell over. His pants split and a flesh-toned tail burst from beneath the fabric and unfurled from his back side. Clear spikes waved like short pennants as the tail whipped around the room. A spasm rolled down his back spines, popping up from each vertebrae. Each wave of transformation brought new agony. His toes burst out of the end of his shoes, black claws formed and clicked on the linoleum.

"Oh, I don't like the next part," Connor said. Standing up he stretched his arms behind his back.

"Is there a way to stop it?" John asked. His arms dislocated and twisting out of its natural state. Elbows protruding forward. Ebony talons now replaced fingers. The color seeped up the scales like spilled ink on parchment.

"Yes, It can be stopped," Connor said. "But I can't help you."

"What about a deal?" John cried.

"Maybe." Connor stroked his chin. "It'd have to be good."

"I know where the contract is," John said. He screamed, his

field of vision shifted and he turned his head to keep Connor in his line of sight. He snorted, tail flailing about the kitchen, floor splintering beneath the mass.

"That's something," Connor said. "But it's still a big ask. What else you got."

John fell to the floor writhing and shrieking. His back legs clawing at the ground chunks of cement denting the wall. Cerebus darted from by the stove to the cold storage door. He scratched at the door prying it open and slipping into the dark.

"I can see you are in a spot of pain. So let's see if we can speed this along," Connor said. He tapped his foot. "Why not lend me your name?"

"What? No," John said. He clenched his eyes closed. Tears streaming in rivulets over the scales forming on his cheeks.

"You did learn something." Connor's head rocked back and forth. "Fine. The contract is enough."

"Make it stop." John's bones cracked, rolling, and shifting into a new alignment. He rolled up like a millipede trying to contain the pain.

"I can't," Connor said. "It all comes down to The Hag's still beating heart."

"Riddles and pain don't mix, Connor," John growled from the ground.

"Hmph, I can't tell you." Connor's face contorted as if smelling something foul. "I even made it easy considering your current state."

"Thanks. I think," John felt as if his insides were bubbling. "I'm going to die."

"Nah. This is worse than death," Connor said. John's tail flew towards the fridge Connor jumped on running down the tail like a bridge, jumping off and grabbing the edge of the white cupboard door by the cold storage. "Then again, if your heart gives out, you will die."

John snapped his head up. "The Hag has to die." John snarled, and whimpered as his face extended into a long narrow snout.

"No moss on you," Connor said. "Now, tell me where the

contract is." Connor straddled the cupboard door as if about to ride into battle.

"Where you can't go," John said. His heart racing, short quick breaths stole his words.

"How specific of you." Connor stood up he balanced on the edge of the door tight rope walking along the top.

"You like riddles," John said. He groaned back arching like a cat, spikes hitting the light.

"Counter offer then." Connor continued along the top of the cupboard door hopping on to the windowsill. "Get the contract for me and I'll be free to help you with The Hag."

John grunted, "You'll help me kill her?"

Connor nodded.

John stretched a clawed hand forward opening the cold storage door. His front half made it through but he had to wiggle his massive hindquarters through the door frame, it splintered and cracked white paint flaked off and fell like snow. Hardened scales scraped against the shelves, mason jars shattered, the smell of vinegar filled the space and his new claws slipped and clinked in the mess on the concrete floor. He needed to escape the myriad of rotten odors in the small space.

He stumbled through the hole in the wall trying to walk down the stairs. He fell forward, four awkward limbs, like an infant trying to crawl, tumbling and tripping down the stairs. He head butted the heavy stone door, skittering across the floor.

Something else scampered in the dark running in and out between his legs, chirping in the dark. Cerebus. *Stupid hodag.* But at least he wasn't alone in the dark. Shadows moved and shifted in his sight. A spectrum of grays, color had disappeared. The chains above creaked, bits of stone clattered, claws and talons clinking over the floor too many sounds. His bones felt as if they were cracking and leaking fire, he felt like tearing himself out of his skin, well scales. John chomped and gasped trying to breath, and then it all faded away.

21

MEANWHILE

Lilith didn't like to be watched and that was exactly what Lisa had been doing. John had gone off to get food and by the time he got back she planned on making Lisa disappear. The dragon's tooth had already been extending her life. As far as Lilith was concerned the girl was already dead. She waited until John's car disappeared around the corner and turned towards the hedge that Lisa was currently trying to hide behind. She made a quick note in her journal about Lisa's presence.

"You can come out now," Lilith said. She started walking down the sidewalk.

Lisa stepped out from behind the hedge and then crossed her arms over her chest as if trying to block Lilith's way.

"Is there a reason you're following me?" Lilith asked. She walked away from her towards her house. *One, two, three...* Lilith counted in her head waiting for Lisa to follow.

"I'm not following you," Lisa said as she caught up to Lilith like a lost child. "I'm keeping an eye on John."

"Stalking," Lilith said. "You're stalking John." She took a left and walked along the gravel driveway, rocks skittering beneath her feet. She stepped up the concrete steps to the front door. The screen door squeaked as she opened it. Pushing the front door open she went inside.

Lisa stood outside on the front porch. She flung her long dark brown braid over her shoulder.

"Come on in," Lilith said. She had left the front door open. "It'll be easier to keep an eye on me."

"No. I think I'll go find John." Lisa stepped down off the porch.

"He'll be back soon enough, he went to grab food," Lilith said. She leaned in the doorway. "Hopefully enough to share."

Lisa came back up the steps and looked over Lilith's shoulder. "Is Iris home?"

Lilith shrugged. "No."

"Good." Lisa headed inside the house and took a seat on the couch.

Lilith shut the door and turned the deadbolt with a click. "You saw what I did in the shed last night. Aren't you scared?"

"I'm worried about keeping John safe," Lisa said. Her hands wrapping around her purse. "There is a great big world out there filled with all kinds of horrors."

"And you're one of them," Lilith said. She sat down on the wing chair across from her, leaning forward she asked. "How much blood have you fed the tooth?"

Lisa sat up straight. "Aren't you frank," Lisa said. "A lot. What kind of tooth is it?" she asked.

"Dragon," Lilith said. "And I thought I had them all locked away."

"Right," Lisa rolled her eyes. "At least you gave me an answer. Iris keep trying to make a deal for information."

"Yeah, I wouldn't make deals with Iris," Lilith said. "There is always a catch."

A car pulled into the driveway engine purring.

"Is that John?" Lisa asked.

"Probably," Lilith said. "Iris doesn't drive." Lilith got up and looked out the big bay window. John had got out of the car and held a big bag of burgers. She licked her lips. She heard a click behind her and felt the muzzle of a gun in her back.

"Really?" Lilith asked. She turned around to face Lisa. "I don't have time for this." She needed to make sure that John made it downstairs. Otherwise she could have a dragon on the rampage in American Fork. She giggled at the thought.

"What's so funny?" Lisa asked.

"Nothing." She walked past Lisa and headed into the kitchen.

"Where do you think you're going?" Lisa asked. She followed behind her.

"To get a drink." Lilith turned on the tap the water rushing out and down the sink. She pulled a glass from the cabinet and filled it. "Would you like some water?"

"No," Lisa said. Her brow knitted in frustration.

The floor shook and something in the basement splintered.

"What was that?" Lisa asked.

"John," Lilith said. "Sounds like I'll have to redo the kitchen." Lilith moved towards the glass sliding door. A hollow scream came from below. Lilith cringed. John was transforming and she knew this part hurt. *Still better than eating him.* She turned and smiled at Lisa.

"I really need to go check on John," Lilith said.

"What have you done?" Lisa asked. She held the gun steady trained on Lilith's chest.

"Do you want to come see?" Lilith asked. "I'm sure John is hungry." She took a couple of steps toward Lisa. She would make a decent snack for the dragon downstairs.

"I know it looks like a toy," Lisa said. She had a steady hand trained at Lilith's chest. "But if it worked on Sarah it'll kill you too."

"I'm not worried about that." Lilith turned her back on Lisa and went to open the sliding door. She figured she could lead her downstairs and into the halls. She tugged on the door it rattled as she tried to open it.

"Come on," Lilith turned around to face Lisa, "put the gun away. We can share stories about killing the ones we love. You would've shot me by now if you were going to go through with it."

Lisa snarled like a leopard and lined up her shot. Lilith now looked down the barrel of the gun. *Give me a knife any day or an honest brawl.*

"I'm glad we're in the kitchen," Lisa said.

"Why?" Lilith asked.

"Because this will make quite a mess." Lisa fired.

Lilith was dead again.

"Not again." Lilith rubbed the back of her head. Her brain pulsing in her skull. This headache would last for days.

"You've made quite the mess of my kitchen, Hag," Iris said. She stood over Lilith hands on slim hips and lips pursed.

"Sorry." Lilith pulled herself up off the linoleum, heading for the sink. "I'll clean it up."

"Make sure you do." Iris opened a drawer and pulled out a dishrag slamming it closed. She tossed it at Lilith.

Lilith cringed the noise reverberating through her skull. "Did you see where the girl went?"

"Who?" Iris asked.

"Oh, please. The one with the dragon's tooth," Lilith said. "You always had sticky fingers when it came to the teeth of my nephews."

"Cain's sons had wonderful bones," Iris said. She smiled, her eyes glittering as if reminiscing. "Beautiful to work with and so easy to shape and carve. I don't suppose you have any more? Downstairs perhaps?"

"Talk to me when you return the bones you've already stolen." Lilith stumbled over to the sink turning on the water and sticking her head under the faucet.

Iris laughed. "You would have to prove it was me, dear. But you may want to make a note. I overheard Lisa confessing to killing Sarah."

"I knew there was a reason I didn't like her." She squinted at the old woman. She pulled out her journal and made a quick note. Splayed across the floor and splattered on the glass were small chunks of gray matter speckled with blue blood. The light of the setting sun casted blue shadows over the floor like stained glass.

Lilith stumbled over and peeled the first piece off the floor. It jiggled between her fingers. She dropped it in her mouth and choked the fluffy paste down. She gathered the little flecks of matter and shoved it into her mouth. Salt and fat fluff rolled over her tongue. She felt relief when she tasted iron.

Iris's face contorted, her nose scrunching up. "That is abhorrent."

"Waste not want not," Lilith said. Walking back over to the sink soaking the dishcloth in cold water. She headed back over to the sliding door. She wiped down the glass, then sucked the blood out of the cloth. She repeated the process until clear water beaded on the glass. "That will have to do."

"You have a funny idea of clean," Iris said. "When that dries the window will be nothing but streaks and the floor won't be much better."

"Let me go deal with the dragon and I'll come back and clean this up," Lilith said. She began tearing up the dishcloth into bite size chunks and choking them down.

"You best bring another tea towel to replace the one you ate." Iris crossed her arms.

"Alright, alright. Dragon, tea towel, and I'll leave the windows and floor streak free." Lilith opened the sliding door. A cold wind stirred leaves on the back porch that skittered in the dying light of the day. She stepped outside.

Iris followed her out, "And before the new moon."

"Yeah, yeah," she said like a child wanting to avoid taking out the trash. She had a messy business to deal with below first.

22

NAKED AND AFRAID

A wet tongue trailed across John's cheek. The saliva should have melted his skin, but it didn't. He wiped away the slime from his cheek flicking it to the ground. John ran his hands down his backside, no tail. Cerebus clawed at his arm. "Ow," John said. "At least I don't have scales." He double checked his arms. Bonus the snout was gone. *I wonder if everything is back where it should be?* He double-checked that he was still male. He was.

Cerebus's claws clicked on the stone floor.

John's butt hurt from the cold. He couldn't see much in the dark. He pulled himself up on the shelf, stumbling forward he stubbed his toe on a loose bit of rock. Cerebus twisted back and forth between his ankles. "Come on boy. Let's get out of here. Maybe I can find something to wear before I get upstairs."

The rate he was losing shirts was getting out of hand. John had no idea where he and Cerebus were he felt like he was lost in an underground labyrinth.

He used the shelf to guide him along, the spines of books bound in dragon leather. Were all of these journals transformed humans? He tried not to think of the hundreds of journals he was passing. He wanted to get away. This wasn't a library it was a crypt.

Running, he needed to run. Feet slapping on the ground, he took off down the hall. Cerebus trotted along beside him, panting in the dark.

His shoulder slammed into a door. His fingers searched to find a crack. Finally his groping hands found their mark and he pulled at the edge of the door. After a struggle, he pulled it open. The sound of scraping echoed in the room.

A faint blue light coated the space. John blinked and he saw the walls were covered in more journals. The darkness seeped down from the ceiling. The far wall was covered in wooden boxes but his eyes landed on a single glowing box. It was the same one that Lilith had put away earlier.

"Hello?" a voice called from the box.

John stopped. "I'm going mad." He rubbed his temples. "Physically I'm fine, but Lilith has destroyed my mind."

"Trying staring at wood grain for centuries," the voice replied. "Then we can talk about going mad."

"I'm going to turn around and run the other way," John said. Cerebus sniffed the floor leading straight for the box on the table. "Come on, boy. Let's go." He followed the hodag toward the box.

"Hold on," the box said. "I can get you out of here. I can't do much. If that makes you feel any better."

"No it doesn't. I was a dragon. Now I'm naked. Talking to a wooden box." John lifted the lid on the box. A skeleton grinned up at him. "The smile doesn't help."

"Would you turn around," the voice said. "Please don't knock the box."

John turned his elbow knocking the box. An image of an old man flickered and refocused like a tube television's picture coming into focus.

"Who the hell are you?" John asked. He dropped his hands over his crotch.

"The only company you have at the moment," the man flickered as he spoke.

John tried to get a good look at him but when he tried to focus on him, he faded from sight. "Wait, are you naked?" the man asked.

"Yes," John said. "I think I may have already mentioned that." John stepped back from the box.

"You were in the middle of turning into a dragon?" The man asked.

"Yes." John held his arm. "Now I'm not."

"Then Lilith has died." The man nodded.

"Not the first time this week." John leaned back, the stone shelf dug into his shoulder. Cerebus waited by the door tail whipping across the floor.

"Let's get you two out of here." The man stared at the boxes behind John. "Before the others start waking up."

"Others?" John asked. "You know what, no. I don't want to know. Lead the way out of here." He headed towards the door.

"You'll need to grab the box." The man crossed his arms. "If you don't mind."

"I mind." John edged closer to the door. "Who are you?"

"A dead man. But I can get you to the exit." The man put a hand on the dark wooden box.

"What's the price?" John asked eyes narrowing. John didn't like the idea of losing the only light he had but he could take his chances in the dark if he had too.

"You carry the box to the next hall. I don't have to listen to the others yak while Lilith regenerates," The man said. "Your naked backside and ugly dog will be out of here."

"I'll ignore your disparaging remark about Cerebus," John said. He moved towards the box. Cerebus right at his heels whimpering as he followed.

John stopped, his hands hovered above the box. "If I touch the box will you be able to steal my body?"

"I would if I could." The figure flickered again.

John stepped back from the box. The hodag gave a low growl stepping towards the ghost.

"I can't steal your body," the man said. "I talk and glow."

John took a deep breath air whistling out as he exhaled. He

picked up the box. Nothing. "Right. Which way?" He gripped the box to his gut, coarse wood grain catching on the hair of his stomach. "Ow, I better not get a splinter."

The blue light flickered ahead of him like static electricity. "You know you would've made it out of here if you had gone right instead of left," The old man said.

"I'll keep that in mind." John shifted the box. Skull rattling against the wood. The hall stretching out in front of them. "Are you another Lilith minion?" he asked.

"No. She can't see me." He stood waiting for John at the next archway. Cerebus circling around the specters feet like a shark.

"Why not?" John asked.

"Lilith can't see the dead." He turned away continuing down the hall.

"Why does she have your skull in a box?" John had to pick up the pace to keep up with the fading figure.

"I use to be someone important to her. She's a little strange." The man smiled a dimple appearing on his right cheek.

"No kidding," John frowned. "The dragon skull in the front room. Human?"

"Yep. Poor bastard. Screeched for days." He appeared next to John.

Goosebumps traveled up his leg, his jaw chattering. "Will she try to change me again?"

The figure paused as if stuck in thought, "She can't. May try to kill you though."

"Figures," John said. "I'll need to prevent that."

"Tell her you saw me. That'll do it." He faded in and out like a shadow.

"Why can I see you?" John asked.

"Don't know." The large dragon skull appeared, the remainder of its skeleton stretched out and disappeared in the dark. Cerebus darted between the bones. Stopping in the skull to gnaw on the mandible. John placed the box down on the heavy table.

"Put the lid back on before you leave," The figure twisted and shifted like smoke from a dying campfire. Can you tell her something?"

"Depends." John put the lid on the box. "I'm not really on speaking terms with her at the moment."

"Tell her I'm sorry." The light disappeared.

John didn't want to go upstairs without the contract, let alone naked.

The chained chandeliers above lit up illuminating the room. Lilith placed a lit torch in the holder by the door.

"You are not a dragon," Lilith said. She smiled walking towards him. The flames crackling above threw long lean shadows across the room.

John backed away from her, hitting the stone shelf behind him with a thud. He grabbed a journal, preparing to defend himself. He didn't like how Lilith looked at him.

She tilted her head looking at him like a crow inspecting carrion. "This is wonderful," Lilith said. She ran over to him, engulfing him in her arms.

John flailed his arms. "Get off of me!" Smacking her in the shoulder with the journal he held.

Cerebus charged out of the mouth of the dragon skull. Snarling he lunged towards them. John grunted as Lilith pushed him behind her. The hodag landed on her chest ripping through her shirt. Lilith pulled her knife out from behind her back. Cerebus whipped his tail around knocking the blade from her hand, clattering as it fell on the ground.

"Cerebus! Down now!" John was more worried about the hodag getting hurt than Lilith.

The hodag paused and dropped to the ground. He circled John three times and then plopped at his feet.

The scratches across Lilith's bare chest began stitching up, as if an invisible needle was repairing a torn piece of cloth. "Great. Now I need a new shirt," Lilith said. "And what is a hodag doing down here?" She headed over to the desk, opening a drawer, she rummaged around inside, pulling out a large old dirty button down shirt.

"Give me that," John moved across the floor attempting to snatch the shirt from her hand.

"No." Lilith held the shirt to her chest. "Get your own."

"I had my own," John said. "But lost it when you tried to turn me into a dragon."

Cerebus play bowed and chirped, nipping at John's ankles.

John made another lunge for the shirt. Lilith dodged. But John caught the tail of the shirt in his hand. He fell to the ground pulling Lilith down on top of him.

"Give it to me," Lilith said. Straddled across John tugging up on the shirt.

John pulled down on the shirt. "I'm cold and naked."

The two continued to bicker like children over a toy. John's arm began tingling the hairs on his arm charging with static electricity.

"Of all the unholy unions!" Zech stood in the doorway, fists clenched. "What are you doing?"

John stood up, Lilith tumbled off him letting go of her half of the shirt. John grabbed the shirt using it to cover his crotch. "Nothing," he said. His cheeks flushed a bright red.

"Nothing?" Zech asked. "Then why are you blushing?"

"Because I'm naked and it's her fault." John said pointing at Lilith.

A vein in the side of Zech's forehead pulsed.

"Not like that, she gave me a potion, and I got big, and naked," John stammered.

Zech had now turned a violent shade of red. The air near him began to crackle. His nostrils flared, "Explain."

John paused. He put the shirt on, fabric itching his shoulder blades. It was long and hung down to his thighs. He took a deep breath. "She gave me a potion. I started to transform into a dragon. A really big dragon. I woke up naked in the dark. When you showed up she was stealing my shirt."

"You mean my shirt," Lilith said.

"You owe me at least four," John spat.

Zech pulled his lips in over his teeth. "I thought she wasn't your type?" Zech asked.

"She's not," John said.

"Hold on," Lilith said. She held up her hands as if calling a timeout. "Who are you?"

"No one you'd remember," Zech said. He pouted folding his arms over his chest.

"How did you know where we were?" John asked.

"Iris told me Lilith was entertaining a gentleman friend." Zech glared at John. "I can see I'm interrupting." The angel moved towards the ornate box on the desk lifting the lid.

"There was nothing to interrupt!" John exclaimed.

"Methinks he doth protest too much," Zech said, inching closer to the table.

John groaned throwing his arms in the air. "Oh, for crying out loud," he said rolling his eyes.

Lilith picked up her blade from where it had fallen on the floor. "Stay away from that."

"I'm only going to borrow it," Zech said. He pulled out the skull holding it up in one hand.

Lilith prowled around the table putting herself between him and the exit. "No."

Zech smiled. "You've never told me no before."

"We've never met before," Lilith scowled.

Great now I'm trapped, again. John edged along the wall trying to put space between him and the quarreling couple. He could make out Cerebus's yellow eyes peering out from behind the teeth of the dragon skull.

Lilith lunged for the skull. Zech spun back but the skull fell from his hand. Cerebus darted out, snatching the skull before it hit the ground and disappearing out the door.

"I will eat that hodag when I catch him," Lilith said. She went to follow him when Zech grabbed her round the waist. "Let go of me," Lilith said. She elbowed him in the gut and he doubled over falling to the ground.

While Zech and Lilith tussled. John slipped out running up the stairs after the hodag. Cerebus sat in the middle of the destroyed kitchen, his wagging tail clearing the debris. He gnawed on the skull like a pup with a tennis ball. None of the clan where anywhere to be seen.

"Give me that," John said.

The hodag darted away. John chased after him, his shirt flapping as he ran. "Cerebus! Now is not the time to play!"

The skull sat in the middle of the front room, smiling, and covered in slobber. Cerebus had given up his prize for something better. Lilith's journal was now in his mouth as he sat on the couch chewing away.

John scooped Cerebus up and then picked up the skull, the drool coating his hand. He opened the door and escaped into the crisp air.

23

BLACKEN HER NAME

I ris chuckled.

John ran down the street, in nothing but a long-tailed shirt, skull in one hand, hodag in the other. She smirked, admiring the view. *Lucky lad, kept all his parts.* She headed back to the kitchen, out the sliding glass door, and down the stairs. Her long tan skirt swished as she went. She hoped the frustrated angel she sent ahead would distract The Hag.

A stroke of luck that he came calling, again.

She opened the door and peeked her head into The Hag's lair. To her, the apartment was also her family's prison.

She would remedy that.

Iris crept down the hall like a field mouse, hoping to catch a glimpse of Connor, even now. Seeing Agnes would also lift her spirits. Though someone should have already stopped her. No one would risk breaking their word and spending their remaining days as a human.

Large gashes cut across the kitchen floor. Iris chose each step with care, bits of concrete crunching beneath her feet. *Last thing I want to do is break a hip.* A peal of thunder rolled through the basement. She giggled as she opened the door to the cold storage, heading down the stairs. Thunder always made her think of the angel she left on the ice float during the clan's crossing over the Atlantic. He deserved it after all his talk of eliminating abominations.

She had arranged for him to be somewhere abominable.

Her thoughts darkened as she descended. The fear of that encounter led her to make a deal with The Hag. Anything to keep the clan safe. Fear also made Connor broker a new deal to save his mother, trapping the clan.

Iris's knees ached, groaning only inside her head, she continued on. She missed being small, bright and colorful. She felt thin, like a film of scum across the top of a pond. Now her skin had a faint yellow undertone. In her true form, Iris had been a vibrant goldenrod. Being old and human was adding insult to injury.

Iris reached a large stone door decorated with carvings. She admired the thistle carved in the corner, it meant death awaited any of the clan who passed through these doors. *Death is one thing I don't fear.* She slipped in through the open door. The first time she tried to get into the halls, it took her hours of prying even with her fairy strength. *Unlike The Hag to be so careless.*

Opening up before her, the hall with flaming chandeliers hanging high above, smelled of iron. One of the few advantages of being human was that iron would not harm her. Her last attempt lead her deep into the halls. She saw all sorts of treasure and even managed to knick a dragon's tooth. She doubted The Hag would leave the contract in the same place.

Iris took a moment to orient herself in the room. She glanced up to the vaulted ceilings, that is a lot of iron. It would not be easy to get up there either. Everything in here seemed designed to keep the clan away from the ceiling. *Up, we go then.*

She climbed the rickety ladder near the door, taking slow breaths to help steady her trembling hands. *I'll have to worry about more than a hip if I fall from this height.* Once on top of the shelf, she used the wall to steady herself. She smoothed her hands over her white collared blouse. No time to go back upstairs and change. Rough rock scrapped beneath her fingers as she moved along.

A flash of light and a clatter came from below. Edging her way to the brink of the shelf, she took a peek below. The Hag and the angel duking it out like two Rock'em Sock'em robots. They stood locked in combat, sword of light in the hand of the angel, dragon bone in the hand of The Hag.

"At least I don't thrash about in my sleep." The angel said, his words drifting up to Iris. He broke free, throwing The Hag into a shelf. Journals scattered and pages fluttered like butterfly wings as they fell to the ground.

"What kind of weirdo watches someone sleeping?" The Hag picked up one of the journals with her free hand, hurling it towards him.

"Really we should give it a break and go after John." He caught the journal before it smacked him in the head. "Then we can go back to killing each other, or whatever else you decide you'd rather do."

"The last thing I want is some crazed angel going after my friend." The Hag charged forward, clutching the dragon-rib like a bat.

"Looked like more than a friend to me." The angel ducked and side-stepped. The rib impacting against the floor with a loud crack, echoing through the space.

"That would be none of your business." The Hag dropped the bone and punched him in the face.

Iris chuckled. They quarreled like jilted lovers. They'd keep each other distracted long enough for her to find what she sought.

She reached the first arch that blocked her way. The chains of the chandeliers creaking next to her. The Hag liked to hide things in plain sight. She pushed on the rocks nothing shifted or moved. "Never a clue when you need one," she muttered under her breath.

The chains shuddered. They made a haphazard web across the ceiling, the chandeliers sitting like black widows waiting for prey. A few of the chains hung low, like a rope lattice that disappeared into the darkness above.

Iris gripped one of the chains giving it a good tug, it held. She placed her other hand on it and stepped on the loop. Knuckles white, she rocked back and forth, reaching out for the next loop.

The entire ceiling quivering as she made her way up into the darkness. The loops made a pathway into the recesses of the ceiling.

Iris steadied herself, ignoring her aching joints. Her focus consuming the pain.

She reached the top of a ladder made from iron leading into a dark hole. Iris grabbed the first rung, her fingers betraying her. She slipped, grasping, and clawing at the chains around her. They tangled and cut at her when she stopped. She felt like a fly wrapped up in webbing ready to be consumed.

The Hag looked up. Iris held her breath, could she be seen?

The angel took the distraction and tackled The Hag around her waist taking her to the ground. The rib fell from The Hag's hand with a clatter. The two tumbled across the floor in a flurry of limbs.

That may be the only time I'll ever be grateful to an angel. Iris untangled herself and made another attempt at the ladder. This time, she managed to climb up. When she reached the top, she skulked over the edge into a hand carved alcove. Flickers of light from below lit up the space, stark shadows stretching across the craggy gray walls. Iris standing, put a hand on the ceiling to keep herself from bumping her head and caught her breath.

Rough-hewn shelves were carved into the walls. A faint kaleidoscope of white and blue light danced on one of the shelves like a shooting star. Iris darted towards it. An array of ornate carved dragon bones lay littered across the shelf.

No harm in grabbing one. She shook her head. During the last attempt she made at getting the contract, the bones distracted her. She spent hours examining them and puzzling out their uses. So distracted in her study, The Hag had been able to pick her up by the collar.

Not this time. Eyes forward, she ignored the bright blue light of the bottles frothing and foaming. The liquid inside them spinning like they contained all of creation. Her nose crinkled at the sight of the iron stoppers on the bottles. Everything in this space had been made to distract her. Contract first, then maybe she could grab something on the way out. The Hag would not miss a trinket or two.

But where to begin? So many trinkets, baubles, and shiny things. A large pile of iridescent stones in hues of blues and purples tempted her to take a closer look. Vessels on another shelf with elaborate gold filigree were large enough to hold the document. She tilted one over to look inside, empty.

A dusty pile of parchment, sitting like a pile of fall leaves in the corner caught her attention. The papers were so plain and ordinary, nothing glittery or shiny about them. She knelt down, rummaging through the pile, tossing sheets of paper into the air. At the very bottom of the pile, lay a stack of papers bound in iron.

Her fingers traced over the circular metal seal emblazoned with a spiky thistle. She hoisted the document up, cradling it like a baby. She now faced a new problem, how to carry it out. Making it up here sapped almost all her strength. Trying to do the same journey back down with the extra weight and one less limb was beyond daunting.

She cursed herself for not thinking to bring a satchel. The fact that she made it up in a skirt was an impressive feat.

It would be easier to climb down if I wasn't wearing the blasted thing. Iris grinned.

She pulled off the skirt, slipping the contract inside, tying the two ends together, and throwing it over her shoulder. Hands on her hips, standing in her granny panties and collared shirt, she prepped herself to make the climb back down.

Good thing I wore underwear today. She snuck back to the entrance, down the ladder, past the quarreling couple, and up the stairs.

Untying the knot in her skirt, she pulled out the contract.

Iris held freedom in her hands. Tears welling up in her eyes, she slipped her skirt back on. One broken seal and the clan would roam again. All the terms, conditions, restrictions, and rules would be void if the seal were released. The Hag should have done a better job of hiding it.

She could not wait to tell everyone. Hugging the contract to her chest, she made her way outside.

Refreshing cold air enveloped her. Spinning and laughing she all but skipped across the yard.

The gate opened, and a large man entered the backyard. "You look like a fairy dancing about like that." He sneered.

Iris looked him up and down. She remembered him. "Nice to see you made it off the iceberg, Gabe. Tell me, were you rescued or did you have to swim home?" Nothing would shatter her good mood, not even a homicidal angel.

Gabe's eyes bulged, jaw clenched, and he rushed Iris.

Iris stepped aside and with a helpful shove, Gabe tumbled forward, face-planting in the dying grass. He pounded a meaty fist against the ground, growling as he got back up.

Iris did not have time for this, as much fun as it was to toy with the brutish lout. She had to get the seal broken before The Hag realized she had it.

Gabe pulled out a thick rope.

"What do you plan to do with that? We don't have enough folk to play double-dutch." Iris stepped back. She wanted out of his reach.

Gabe roared, flailing the rope. A ripple of thunder pealed out across the sky.

Iris's skin prickled. "You know I'm human now. No longer an abomination."

"Once an abomination always an abomination." Gabe snapped the rope.

An idea percolated in her mind. The strength of this brute could solve two of her problems.

24

GOLDEN YEARS

"*What am I doing down here?*" Lilith rubbed her head. The chandeliers glittered with light, but she couldn't remember why she came down. Had she fallen down the stairs again? Wasn't the first time.

Her encounter with Lisa filtered into her mind. Right, John should have finished transforming by now. Did John get her? She checked herself for claw marks and bites.

No dragon marks, but a scar branching out like lighting from her chest and up her neck appeared fresh, still tender. At least she managed to keep her bra this time.

The stone door to the main hall lay on the floor, cracked in two. Heading up the stairs, she expected to find a dragon wedged between the ceiling and walls. "He should have been too big to fit out the door," she muttered.

But there was no dragon in the hall.

He wasn't in the kitchen either.

"Connor!" No answer. "Connor, where are you? Have someone bring me a shirt would ya?"

"I'm coming." Connor appeared on top of the fridge.

"Where were you?" Her eyes narrowed, fingernails drumming on her arm.

"Hunting nemas." Connor shrugged. "Like you asked."

Lilith could tell he was leaving something out, but John was the more pressing concern. "Have you seen a Dragon?"

"Once or twice. You'll have to be a little more specific." Connor disappeared into the air-duct, its cover hanging loose from the ceiling. "But an angel ran out of here not too long ago."

"How did he get in?"

"Don't know." Connor reappeared on the sink, walking the faucet like a balance-beam. "If you're quick, you may still catch him in the yard."

"We will be having a discussion." Lilith pursed her lips.

"I can only do one thing at a time, Hag." Connor stood on the edge of the faucet arms crossed.

Lilith leanined down, putting herself at eye level with him. "Keeping angels out of my house should be a priority."

"Do you want to catch him or not?" Connor turned around walking back down to the back of the sink.

Lilith threw her arms up in the air.

Running down the hall, she picked up a discarded shirt. "Add the kitchen to your fix-it list," she called before leaving.

Charging up the external stairs, Lilith found Iris fighting with Gabe over a large document, the size of a fantasy epic.

"The contract?" Lilith gaped. "Guess I didn't leave enough distractions and traps after all."

"Hello, Hag. Took you long enough." Iris stood on the far side of the wrecked yard. She ducked as a glowing rope cracked over her head, retracting back to the angel by itself.

Gabe turned around. "Abomination!" He strangled the thick rope, likely pretending it was her neck.

"Good to see you too." Lilith could not lose the contract. The dragon would have to wait. "Iris, you've been where you shouldn't."

"True," Iris agreed.

Gabe cracked the rope like a whip towards Lilith. Vibrations coursed through the air rattling her.

"Give me the contract and I'll save your hide." The rope

careened towards Lilith's ankles. She jumped over it, running over to Iris's side.

"No." Iris stepped away from Lilith, towards Gabe. "I thought you'd be more concerned about John."

"John is gone," Lilith grabbed Iris by the shoulders moving her out of the way of another one of Gabe's wild attacks, the ground shaking beneath her feet. "Being a dragon kind of murders the human side."

"True, but he's not a dragon anymore. At least not the bits I saw." Iris wiggled her eyebrows.

Lilith stopped, her heart feeling another strange emotion. "He's not dead." Lilith no longer hungered for his blood. Lisa shooting her in the head actually did some good. "Where is he?"

"Probably chasing after the loony that blasted your brains out." Iris's knuckles turned white from clutching the contract.

Gabe bull-rushed the two women. "Neither of you will have to worry about any of that."

Lilith shifted back, after letting him pass. "Why would that be?"

"Because, Zech will catch him soon enough." He lunged for Iris.

Iris tripped over one of the mounds of dirt, caused from the tank explosion, and she fell to the ground.

"I'll be killing the fairy and taking you to Cheri," Gabe said.

"Yeah, no." Lilith threw her shoulder into him knocking him away from Iris.

"I didn't know you cared," Iris smirked standing, brushing off the dirt, and holding the contract in one arm.

"I don't. You have family that cares about you and I don't need the earache that would come from you dying."

The ground gave way beneath their feet. Lilith yanked Iris to safety.

Gabe doubled the rope, twisting it above his head. Lassoing the two of them, tying a hitch knot, cinching it, before securing them.

"It's Gabe, right? Here's a thought, why don't we lay off this whole murder, death, kill thing?" Lilith gasped. Fighting to breathe as air pushed out from the tightening bonds.

"Not a chance, abomination," Gabe said.

Lilith wriggled against the contracting ropes. "Can we drop the whole 'abomination' thing? You act as if somehow it's all my fault." Lilith grunted, ropes burning into her skin.

Iris went slack against her back, her snippy comments silenced.

Gabe pushed in close, nose to nose with Lilith. "This world contained no unnatural creatures before your betrayal."

Lilith's back arching, vertebrae popping, she dropped to the ground and out of the ropes. Placing her hand on the ground, she steadied herself. "Good to know."

Gabe grabbing her by neck and hoisted her up. "You are responsible for every single abomination that walks this world. We will find a way to be rid of you."

"It'll take more than a tight grip to get rid of me." She winked, just before clawing at his fingers and stomping the insole of his foot.

Gabe yelped and Lilith scrambled free.

Iris gasped, pulling in air, inching out of the rope like a worm. "You'll want to hurry if you want a chance at saving John. If Zech doesn't get him, Lisa will."

"Leave you alone with the contract? Never." Lilith helped Iris up.

"Don't worry, I'm sure he's already dead." Gabe wrapped his arms around Lilith from behind, crushing her.

Lilith thrashed about in his embrace like a trout trying to escape a grizzly bear.

"I can distract this one." Iris stood up and composed herself, adjusting her shirt. "You'll have to choose, Hag. John or the contract."

Gabe, shifting positions, put Lilith in a choke hold his thick bicep pinning her chin.

John is alive and I need to keep my friend breathing. She would find another way to protect her memories. Lilith closed her eyes and nodded her consent to Iris.

"Tell me, Gabe," Iris began, "considering what I saw of you on the ice, are all the angels lacking below the belt, or is it just you?"

Gabe dropped Lilith.

He held up a hand. The rope on the ground slithering towards him, shaking and twisting. Doubling up the length of the rope before swinging it in arcing circles. He sent the loops flying toward Iris. The rope constricted around her and the contract, like a boa constrictor.

The binding that held the document together snapped under the pressure. The pages fluttering in the air, fell, littering the lawn like so many dead leaves. Iris withered, shrinking to a speck of gold.

Gabe, wrapping the rope up, smiled.

Lilith knew to flee. All the promises, words and magic that Iris contained were about to be released back into the world.

Lilith jumped the short gate, running down the driveway, and away from the house. A brilliant burst of gold glittered across the sky, shock waves of magic rolling out from where the former queen lay.

25

OUT OF THE FRYING PAN

L ilith cursed herself. That was one hell of a distraction that Iris pulled off. *Never one to do something quietly.* She searched her pockets. Where had her journal gone? In her back pocket, a pen and scrap of paper. *Iris dead, contract broken. Save John.* She wrote.

That would have to do until she found her journal. Shoving it back into her pocket, she ran on.

A car roaring down the road behind her interrupted her thoughts. She turned around, the blue vehicle jumped the sidewalk, hitting Lilith in the hip. Pain ruptured on her side and radiated through her guts. The car engine purred next to her, a predator admiring its prey.

The car door opened.

Lilith turned over groaning. Lisa towered over her, hands on her hips. "How?"

"No idea what you could mean," Lilith gasping, grabbed her side. Her arm wrapping around her gut, the other against her shattered hip.

"I shot you in the head." Lisa opened the passenger-side door.

"Yes." Shock waves of pain rolling down her leg. She could feel the arcs of electricity pulsing up her spine.

Lisa grabbing her ankles and flipped her over. "Come on."

The grass crackled under Lilith as Lisa tugged her along. "No thanks, really. I have other things to do."

"You will make an excellent meal." Lisa hoisted Lilith into the car.

"Bad idea." Lilith eyes rolled back, but she fought to stay conscious.

Organs stitching back up, felt like hooks raking her gut. The bone in her leg set out of alignment. She'd have to re-break and set it. Lilith grimaced at the thought.

Her arm still hanging out of the car, Lisa slammed the door on it.

Lilith screamed, the sound muffled by the closed door.

Lisa opened the door, a sadistic smile on her lips. "Oopsies." She pulled at the arm, torquing it at a peculiar angle, fascinated by the flesh healing and the bone knitting at the awkward angle.

"What else can you do?" Her eyes widened.

"I'm not much for party tricks." Lilith gritted her teeth, trying to suppress the pain enough to do something.

"I wanna see what else you can do." Lisa shut the car door. Walking back around the driver's side getting in, she started the car, and peeled off down the road.

"This is a terrible idea." Lilith's head flopped over like a rag doll.

"So, you say." Lisa stopped at the red traffic light.

"Last warning," the words tumbled out of Lilith's mouth. "You're already cheating death. Bringing me into the picture will expedite the debt collecting."

"You keep saying that." Lisa proceeded when the light changed. Indicator clicking, she turned the corner. "Yet, here I am."

"Let me guess, you were terribly sick, injured or maimed as a child? When a kindly old woman, or man, gave you the necklace?" Lilith rolled her head towards Lisa. Lilith suspected that Iris had somehow been involved with the girl getting hold of the tooth.

"No. I found it in a pile of stag bones soaked in blood. Life tends to be better if it stays soaked in sacrificed blood. Animals work, but I discovered it prefers people." Lisa smiled at the road, "And so do I."

Lilith shook her head, surprised. "You feed it death? Your death will be horrid."

"Not as bad as yours will be." Lisa focused on the road.

Lilith rolled her eyes. Time to see whether or not Iris had been telling the truth, "Sarah had my blood. How did you get it?"

Lisa glanced over at her. "I went hunting."

"John will not be happy about that." Lilith scrunched her eyes closed. The past couple of days were catching up with her. Broken necks, blasted brain, shattered bones, and a complete regeneration.

"John doesn't need to know, now does he?" Lisa parked in a driveway outside a contemporary house with river-stone facing. The houses down the streets looked like they all came from the same cookie cutter.

Lilith, trying to keep her eyes open, jabbered on. "Have you tried keeping any promises? Opens up a whole new world of opportunities."

Lisa got out of the car and dragged Lilith out of her seat. "I feed it blood, it gives me strength. For now, I don't need anything else."

Lilith's eyes grew heavy and closed, not dead, but overwhelmed with pain.

Waking up in a plain, sterile room did not bring her any comfort. Large cream straps held her in place. Shimming her hips, the handle of her blade squeaked on the metal table. Right arm pulsing, two new joints pointed in opposite directions. The arm looking like a badly planned roadway and the rest of her still under construction. *Eh, Spanish Inquisition was worse.*

A thumping in her ears beat like a kettle drum. A large needle stuck out of her left arm. Blue blood pumped out of a line leaving her body. *Crap, worse than Spain.*

On the counter, three plastic bottles brimmed with her blood. Lisa leaned next to them, a kid in a candy store.

Being drained meant she felt nothing, she became an empty shell of consumption running amok.

"Oh, good! You're awake." Lisa pirouetted across the room. "I have so many questions for you!"

"Awfully chipper for someone that has a monster strapped to a table." Lilith's mouth felt dry as if filled with cotton.

"It's a great day!" she crossed back over to the bottles snapping off one of the lids. "Can I get you anything juice, milk, water perhaps?"

"Don't suppose I could get that blood back?" Lilith asked, her cheek pressing against the cold metal.

Lisa laughed, putting the container down. "Your blood is good. The pendant loves it."

The container that currently caught her blood began to dribble over the side on to the floor. Lisa came over kinking the line switching out the containers. She lifted the fresh container to her lips.

"Please don't do that." Lilith's head jerked up from the table. "It'll kill you."

Lisa took a swig, licking here lips. "Odd, it's sweet. Way better than most of what I've guzzled over the years." She took another swig. Placing the lid on, she lined it up with the others.

Lilith dropped her head on the table, a loud thunk ringing out in the room. "You're killing me." Closing her eyes, she ignored the cold in her fingers and numbness in her toes.

"You'll come back. I'll never have to kill anyone else." Lisa opened a cupboard and pulled out some supplies.

"When I come back. I won't be as reasonable." Her head throbbing, swimming in and out of consciousness.

Lisa took another swig, her lips stained blue like a child with a lollipop.

"You really should stop that. You don't want to be a monster snack." Lilith muttered, her eyes closing. The line in her arm slowly dripped like an hourglass running out of sand.

26

SANITY CHECK

J ohn stripped out of the old shirt. He sighed as he pulled on his own cotton tee. After pulling on his jeans, he felt like he was back in his own skin. He didn't know where Lilith could be.

But Lisa wouldn't be safe with Lilith on the loose.

"Come on, Cerebus. In you go." John ushered the hodag into his backpack, which contained the skull and Lilith's journal. He laced up his shoes, heading out the door towards Lisa's place.

A flickering of blue light caught John's eye. The hair on his arms stood on end. *Static?* A crackling noise brought him to a stop. When the old man from Lilith's halls appeared in front of him, John swallowed his panic.

"Hello, again." The transparent figure stood, arms-crossed in front of him. eyes wide. "What a treat. I'm outside!"

"Yes. Yes you are." John continued running down the sidewalk. Cursing that in his flight from Lilith's, he left his car behind.

"How long has it been?" The specter asked. He flickered in and out of John's sight line.

"Same day." John huffed, dragging the back of his hand across his forehead, flicking away the sweat onto the sidewalk.

"Yikes," the specter replied, crackling like an old radio.

"Also, I only think it fair to tell you. You're my prisoner." John's sneakers dragged over the pale cement.

"Your prisoner?" The ghost froze, stalling like a buffering YouTube video.

"I'd like to avoid being killed, and you seem important to Lilith. Another girl may also be involved." John wheezed. He made it to the stoplight.

"I'm not the best choice as a hostage." The specter frowned. "This is a bad idea. If Lilith died again today, she's hungry. Your girl may be on the menu."

John crossed the road. He hated running, but since Lilith came along, he did a lot of it.

John headed to Sarah and Lisa's place. Riverstone house with a green door.

"Something is hungry." John's companion leaned on the door, left wide-open. "Can't you feel it?"

"No." John ignored a niggling in his chest, he didn't want to acknowledge. They entered the house.

"This way." The specter blended in with the blue wall behind him.

"Are you sure?" John's shoes squeaked on reclaimed hardwood floors.

"Certain." The voice of the ghost came from down the hall, out of one of the open bedroom doors. John entered the room, pale pastels covering every surface. A large white board hung on the wall, marked with goals and empty check boxes.

"In here," the ghost called from the closet.

"You are messing with me?" John stepped into the walk-in closet. A menagerie of clothes in a spectrum of colors filled every surface. "No way they are in here."

"You idiot." The ghost pointed at the wall behind him. "Lilith is behind that wall."

"Right." John ran his fingers around the edge of the wall, finding nothing.

"Try again." The ghost stared at the wall.

John rammed his shoulder against it and the plaster gave way with a snap.

"Careful, boy." The spirit's head, floating above a lovely blue dress, looked like a stern school marm.

"If you're here Lilith is dead." John pulled the wall out of the way. "What could happen?"

Fluorescent light cascaded out from behind the wall. A hidden room with a toppled medical table and a gnawing noise, like a dog chewing on a bone.

"Don't go in there!" The ghost exclaimed. He reached out as if to pull John back to safety. John shivered at the hand passing through him, jumping away to escape the feeling.

The gnawing stopped, a low growl taking its place.

A long, lean figure with gaunt-hollow eyes climbed over the upended table.

Gray flesh clung onto the bones of the emaciated creature. Dark red hair with clots clinging to the strands hung to her shoulders. A macabre contrast between her ashen skin and the crimson staining the lower half of her jaw. She clutched a femur in her hand. Breaking the bone in two, she sucked the marrow out.

"You need to get out of here." The ghost swept towards her. "She lost too much blood."

The room made no sense with all the medical grade equipment. It looked like the setup of a mortician. On the counter, sat a row of plastic bottles full of blue blood. "What if she got the blood back?" John asked.

"She'd need a lot to eat to regain her sanity." The ghost moved closer to Lilith.

"It'd be nice to save at least one person today." John stepped forward.

"Right now, you are only food." The ghost ran his hand down her back like a parent trying to soothe a temperamental child.

Lilith's head jerked up. The specter growled in a guttural tone. "Brother?"

"Of course, you're her brother." John snuck around the table, heading for the counter.

"Bring it all." The ghost rested his hand on Lilith's shoulder.

"Please don't let her eat me." John popped one of the lids off.

Lilith's head whipped around. Grabbing at the bottle, she downed the blood, eating the container. Her attention turned to John, lining him up in her sights. Like prey.

"Start running." the ghost said, a slow smile spreading across his face.

"Not more running." John booked it out of the house, bottle of blood in hand, Lilith on his heels.

"You need to find her food." The ghost kept pace next to him.

"You don't say?" John glanced over his shoulder.

Lilith dropped on all fours, loping behind them like a great dane.

"Probably not the best way to handle this. I did try to tell you not to go in there." The ghost floated backwards, while John fled for his life.

"Not helping," John said between breaths. *How many times am I 'almost' going to die today?* In the dark, lighting filtered across the sky. "Not more angels."

Zech graced them with his presence. "Quite the pickle you got here."

"What do you want?" John sprinted down the road. Passing work, he headed towards the shopping complex. *He looks like he's sauntering. Not even breaking a sweat.*

"No, I'm not," Zech chortled as they he kept pace. "Would you like some help?"

What's the cost? John couldn't waste his breath on talking. His backpacked growled.

"What is that?" Zech asked.

"Cerebus the hodag," John panted.

The hodag popped his head out of the bag, snarling at the angel.

"I'm not calling him that. He looks like a Spot to me. Would you like some help?"

"What's it going to cost?" John asked.

Zech eyed the bag on his back. "The box and skull in your backpack."

"Don't give me to the damn angel!" The ghost yelled glowing bright blue. "Anyone but him!"

A howl came from behind the three of them, causing John to jump.

"Ah, come on, Cain." Zech looked over at the specter. "It wouldn't be that bad."

"If I wanted to be tormented, I'd go talk to my brother!" Cain exclaimed rolling his eyes.

"Not to interrupt." John strained to pull breath. "But, ravenous, monster, behind me."

"What do you say? Deal?" Zech asked coasting along with no effort. "Box for my help?"

"Yes," John wheezed, grasping at his side.

"Alright!" Zech rubbed his hands together, then pulling them apart, a blade of light appeared.

What are you going to do? John thought.

"I'm going to slow her down." Zech swung the blade through the air.

Wait! John thought pulling deep breaths into burning lungs. *Wouldn't killing her again be a bad idea! She's already died twice today!*

"What have you two been up to?" Zech put the blade away. "I don't think I like how you're influencing my Lilith."

"Your Lilith?" Cain's image sparked.

"Stop bickering and start helping!" John stumbled into the empty parking lot of the shopping complex. "You can sort out the family domestics later. Right now, we need food."

A piercing shriek came from behind them.

"A lot of food." John's feet skidded beneath him. Heading to the right, a barrage of fast food signs lit up the night.

The air charged with static. "Get her to a dumpster and I'll take care of the rest," Zech said, then zipped off before John could reply.

"How do I get her in a dumpster?" There were three in sight, but he didn't think opening one of the green behemoths and inviting Lilith in would work.

"You use live bait." Cain flickered like a dying candle.

"Great idea." John ran towards the closest dumpster behind a steakhouse. "The cops will find my remains in the morning."

"I'm starting to fade. Once she eats, she'll be fine."

"Ah, Hell!" John flipped the lid of the dumpster open, scrambled up the side and tossed himself in, like a piece of refuse.

A variety of smells wafted up at him, initially, old pieces of discarded steak and stale bread, and vegetables. A second wave of putrid smells began to overwhelm him and he looked up, seeking fresh air. Lilith perched on the metal wall. Her neck at an unnatural angle as she watched him.

She scaled down inside the dumpster, feasting on the rejected remains. John wedged himself into the corner, huffing, unable to catch his breath.

"I'll leave you to your meal." John reached up, preparing to pull himself onto the lip. He glanced over his shoulder.

Lilith shuffled towards John sniffing the air. Head bobbing and weaving, back and forth, her face regaining its shape but her eyes still shown like dark pits of nothing.

Can I get out of here before she attacks me? John placed another hand on the edge of the dumpster.

Someone grabbed him, pulling him out of the dumpster.

Zech smiled, giving John a wink. A stack of black trash bags leaned against the fence. "Come on. Help me get these bags in there."

John picked up a bag, gagging as the smell of rotten eggs hit him. He threw it in.

Lilith's long lean fingers wrapped on the ledge of the container, her head popping out of the dumpster like a possessed Jack in the Box.

"More food." Zech picked up a bag, throwing it at Lilith's head. She disappeared.

John sighed. "I don't know if we will be able to keep her in there."

"All we need to do is keep her feeding." Zech hopped up, balancing on the side. He held out his hand for the bottle of blood that John handed over. "I'll go in, rip some bags open, no problem. Close the lid once I'm in."

HAUNT ME EVERYDAY

*Z*ech sighed, and held his breath, and jumped into the high wall dumpster. John shut the lid behind him. The lid didn't quite line up so a large swathe of moonlight cut across the floor. He slipped on a black garbage bag and landed on his butt with a thud. He scrambled back up onto his feet, knee deep in trash. Compared to some of the scrapes he'd been in with Lil this was pretty mild.

She'd only consumed one, maybe two people this time, better than the double digits she had hit in the past.

The light of the moon cut in through the top of the dumpster. Bits of dust danced and swished Zech couldn't see her, but the occasional rustle gave away that Lilith was there.

"Come on, Lil," Zech said. "I've got at least a liter of your blood here." He popped open the container the thick blue blood sloshed in the bottle.

A low hiss came from the far side of the space.

"You don't really want to eat John," Zech said. "He's actually a good kid. He may even be able to help you."

A plastic bag crumpled in the far side of the dumpster. Lilith, on all fours, moved into the moonlight. Gray hair soaked with dark dry blood. Lilith paced back and forth in the moonlight. A variety

197

of smells wafted through the space, stale bread, bad meat. It had been a while since he had been in the presence of something stronger than him. Lilith had always been stronger than him.

A forced half-smile pulled across his face. "There you are," he said. "You are looking a little worse for wear there, love." He held up the container in his hand, making an attempt at trying to be flirtatious he took a few steps forward but his feet stuck in the liquid mash of whatever had been cleared from the tables inside. "Fancy a drink?"

She paced to the right and Zech mirrored her movements. "Blood first and then we will find something for you to snack on," he said. "Steak? I bet there is leftover steak in here somewhere."

Lilith charged, Zech sidestepped and she barreled into the metal wall with a sickening crunch.

He frowned. *Lil had seen too many deaths today, too much blood loss, and too hungry for reason.* She'd be starving for weeks. Lil rolled over and rocked her head side to side in a wide arc, the bones in her neck clicking. Tendons and sinew clung to her frame, a living skeleton. The opalescence of her bones shone from beneath translucent skin.

"I never wanted to lie to you, Lil," Zech said. "I don't want to lie anymore." He took a few steps towards her, sacks of trash crushing beneath him.

Lilith hissed and scampered to the wall behind her trying to claw her way up and out.

Zech grabbed her by the ankle. He could feel the bones moving beneath his fingers, he wanted to be tender with her, like in Pompei, but now wasn't the time. With a sharp tug, he brought her crashing back down into the dumpster grabbing the squirming predator by her shoulders.

"You know I love you, right?" He pinned her across the shoulders with his free arm. Lilith howled, her jaw extending and the paper-thin skin around her jowls tearing.

Zech lifted the bottle to her mouth. "But I've never been able to get it right," he said. Pouring the viscous blood down her throat. "Not even the first time around. I shouldn't have lied to you about what I am, but I thought it was the only way, and I wanted you bad enough to risk it."

She gulped as he poured the contents of the container down her throat. All the monster wanted was to feast. Part of Zech wanted to believe that Lilith could hear him and remember him, the rest knew better, but he wasn't listening to that part. "You have no idea how much it hurts when you tear me out of your life," he said. "I wonder if I were honest and told you everything I knew about us if it would make a difference."

Lilith fed on the empty container, sharp teeth tearing through the plastic.

He stopped himself from touching her, "But you'd reject me if you knew the truth."

Lilith let out a loud burp when she had finished the plastic, even her actions were all honesty.

Zech laughed. "You were always so shocking."

She snarled.

He jumped back tearing more bags open, exposing remnants of leftover meals from the steakhouse. Zech hoped it was late enough that no one else would be around the shopping complex. "I always have to be a little better with you around and, worst of all, you make me think."

Lil paused and watched him as if a memory flickered behind her glassy stare. Her hands full of stale bread rolls, she returned to gorging, making a loud smacking sound as she gobbled them down.

Zech inched closer. "I still want you, in a way that I can't explain. Even like this. But we are horrible for each other," he squatted against the sidewall where years of trash scrapped the blue paint away, leaving the tarnished silver exposed. "I need to be better and so do you."

Used napkins, butter wrappers, and a treasury of empty peanut shells disappeared into Lilith's unending hunger by the handful.

"I don't know which is worse, the fact that I can't forget or that you don't remember," Zech said, mushy tenderness for her filling his mind with all the times they'd followed these same steps in this same dance.

Lillith stood up. Her eyes narrowed as she examined him. Her stride matched that of a tiger, tattered shirt fluttering as she moved towards him, in all her terrible glory.

"Lil?" Zech asked. Did she recognized him? "Are you back?"

She placed her hand on the back of his neck and pulled him close as if to kiss him. Her gray eyes seemed to be searching.

He leaned forward too, hoping for a kiss. He missed being this close.

Instead, she snarled and lunged for his neck.

Zech tried to dodge, but her teeth lodged into the flesh of his shoulder.

"Not back!" Zech yelled as he tried to push the ravenous creature off him. Fire blazed through his arm. Lilith tore the flesh away, chewing, before leaning in to continue. Zech hooked his leg behind hers and swept her onto her back.

Lillith recovered, crouching on the ground. She snarled, licking the crimson blood from her lips. She watched him as if deciding whether or not he was worth the effort of eating, then returned to consuming garbage.

"You're never going to remember me, are you?" he asked. He let his head thump against the metal wall. He winced at the large chunk of his black shirt she ha torn away, the frayed fibers mixed with the torn flesh and blood. Tiny flickers of blue surged between the muscles, like fireflies inside his flesh. He breathed in sharply through clenched teeth. Fire sizzled up his neck and down his arm. He clamped his good hand down on the wound, to stop the blood and contain the pain.

It would heal but he'd need time. "Every time, I hope—" he stopped.

Lilith had taken a bag in her mouth shaking it like a pit bull with a bone. Plastic cups and peanut shells flinging about as if drool clattering against the metal walls.

Zech turned his good shoulder to protect it from the shrapnel.

Lilith turned her back on him.

200

"It drives me mad that you can't remember any of our past."
Zech let go of the wound on his shoulder, pushing up on the heavy
plastic lid it creaked as it opened. He chanced one last glance at
Lilith, she didn't look up.

"You haunt me every day." Zech used his good arm pulling
himself out of the dumpster leaving Lillith to feast.

John stood ready with a bit of pipe he must have had found.
Spot ran around him in circles, obsidian claws clicking on the
ground. Zech limped towards the fence, applying pressure on his
open wound.

"Did she take a bite out of you?" John dropped the pipe which
clinked on the ground. He came over to check on the damage.

"I let her," Zech said. "It'll heal. A bite like this would've killed
you." He leaned against the fence and slid down to the ground.
Watching the dumpster to make sure she stayed inside.

"Thanks for pulling me out," John said. "Seriously though,
what's the deal with you two?" John joined him on the ground.
Spot circled three times and sat down next to him, dark scaly-green
head resting on John's leg.

Zech leaned his head against the fence, looking up at the sky. "I
wish I knew," he said. Closing his eyes, he listened to Lilith rifle
through the dumpster. "May I have the box, please?"

"No," John said. He pulled his backpack off his shoulder.

"What do you mean no?" Zech asked.

John unzipped his bag pulling out Cain's skull wrapped in a
dishcloth. "Box wouldn't fit in my bag." He handed the skull over
to Zech.

Zech chuckled and unwrapped the skull placing it on his
knee. He pushed the cloth to the wound on his shoulder.
"Thanks."

John rifled through his bag and pulled out Lilith's journal.

"Wondered where that had gone," Zech said.

John flipped through the pages frowning as he looked over the
contents of the past couple of days. "Tempted to rip these pages
out," He said. He held three pages between his thumb and index
finger.

Zech jolted upright and Cain's skull tumbled off his leg. "Bad idea!"

"What?" John asked. "If I take these pages out she won't remember me, right?"

"Yep," Zech said. "You'll also cause a catastrophic natural disaster." He picked up the skull and brushed it off.

"Really?" John asked. He let the pages slip free.

"One word," Zech said, holding up his pointer finger. "Pompeii."

"You caused Pompeii?" John demanded. He slammed the cover closed as if he expected it to bite him.

"Inadvertently, sort of," Zech said. "Lilith may have a really good reason for wanting to rip me from her memory. That's normally how it goes with us."

"But, how did she know your name?" John asked. He put the journal back in his bag.

"What do you mean?" He sat forward, interested, but still frowning.

"The first night I met Lilith, she said your name while she was healing," John replied, scratching the scales behind Spot's ear. "Zech is not a common name. I figure she meant you." The gentle clinking noise far more soothing than the continued thrashing of Lilith in the garbage. The hodag nuzzled John's hand.

"I don't know," Zech said. *She remembers me?* Thunder rumbled in the distance. "Playing my song." He stood up, skull in hand.

"You're not going to help me keep an eye on Lilith?" John asked.

"If I don't report in. Other angels will come looking for me," Zech said. "Gabe included. Don't worry, she has plenty of food and she'll pass out before long." He started walking away. "Try to stay alive kid."

28

SYMPATHY FOR THE DEVIL

L ilith's head throbbed like a bad rock ballad. She pulled a black trash bag off her face, crumpling it up and tossing it away from her.

A ray of light seeped in through the top of the dumpster, cutting across the darkness like light across a cathedral floor. But this space wasn't holy, this was where everything no one wanted ended up.

This is the perfect place for trash like me. She shook her head trying to chase the thought away. Instead embracing the desire to talk with John. He might be able to help her figure out what she had learned from Gabe.

If she was the cause of all abominations as he put it. Then maybe it was her responsibility to take care of them. She didn't want the responsibility, but she couldn't let anyone else get hurt. That sort of responsibility sat heavy on her, a coat she'd never worn before. Not exactly uncomfortable, but unfamiliar.

She stared at the lid of the dumpster and considered drifting off, the idea of possibly being picked up and crushed by a trash truck made her try to get moving.

"Ugh," she wiped the spittle away from her lips and pulled a long dark strand of her hair out from beneath her tongue.

Who did that belong to? Her brow furrowed as she recalled last night's entry in her journal was about going out and finding Lisa.

"John! Crap, Lisa is going to kill John!" She stood up and the brown walls of the dumpster seemed to warp around her.

Did I lose blood last night? She stumbled forward pushing up against the heavy black lids of the container. She groaned as the early morning light blasted her. "Got to get to John." Her fingers gripped the cold metal.

"I'm right here," John said. He sat with his back against the fence that surrounded the large dumpster, a decapitated security camera hung by a frayed cable above him. One of his knees could be seen through torn dirty jeans, black shirt tattered, bruises and scrapes covered any visible skin. Curled up by his side, a hodag purred.

"You're alive!" Lilith pulled herself out of the dumpster, slipped, and fell to the ground with a whack. Crawling over to him, she wrapped her arms around him giving him a hug.

It didn't even bother her that John cringed at her touch.

"You stink," she said. "Are you ok?" She grabbed his face in her hands examining it.

He waved her off.

"You look awful. What did this to you? Hodag? Angel?" she asked.

The hodag peered at her with yellow eyes and growled.

"Chill, Cerberus," John said. He scratched between the scales on his head, he settled back down, then in answer to her question, "You."

Lilith flopped down on the ground. "I'm sorry." She pressed her hands to her temples. "The last little bit is foggy." Her head thumped like a box of books tumbling down stairs. The overwhelming taste of sweet chili sauce and garbage filled her mouth. "It tastes like I bit an angel." She wiped her tongue with the back of her hand.

"You took a chunk out of Zech," John scoffed. "I'm sure Cain will have a good laugh when he finds out."

"Who?" Lilith asked.

"You're not-quite-over-you ex," John informed her. "I don't know what he sees in you."

"I don't have an ex named Zech, and Cain is dead," Lilith said, then pointing at him. "Besides, you can't talk to the dead."

"Turns out when you're dead," John said. "They can speak. That skull can jabber."

Lilith's skin prickled. "Where is the skull?" Her fingers scratching at the dirty asphalt.

"Zech has it. He saved my life. Figured it was a fair trade." John crossed his arms over his chest.

"The angels have the box?" Lilith scrambled up to her knees. She gritted her teeth, and frowned. *First the contract now Cain?*

"No," John said. "They have the skull."

"That wasn't yours to trade," Lilith rubbed her face, millions of memories assaulting her mind with the possibilities of what could come next. "The box and dragon blood keep the skull from falling apart." She jabbed him in the chest with her index finger. "You are helping me get it back."

"Ow," John said slapping her hand away. "And no, I'm not." He rubbed at the spot Lilith poked.

"You owe me!" Lilith shook her fist at him.

John thumped his head on the fence, the chain link rattled behind him. "I figured I had some leeway, especially with you trying to turn me into a dragon," John said. "Oh yeah, don't forget your intention of using my skin for journal covers." He opened his backpack and ushered Cerberus inside. The hodag hung his head out of the bag, tongue lolling over his teeth. John stood up and put the bag on.

"Where are you going?" she asked.

"Home," he said and started walking away through the parking lot.

Lilith got up and followed him. "Can I crash at your place?"

John stopped. "No! You can go back to your place."

"I can't," Lilith walked next to him, rubbing the back of her neck.

"Why not?" John adjusted the strap of his bag and continued walking at a brisk pace.

"I had to make a choice," Lilith said. She tried to pull her tattered shirt back up on her shoulder. Then pushed a matted piece of hair behind her ear. "I could save you from Lisa. Or I could keep Iris from the contract."

John slowed down, frowning. "Why would you save me? Doesn't make sense, you made a big deal about how terrible it would be if the clan got loose." Cerberus whimpered and pulled his head inside the backpack.

"Yeah, it's going to be a massive headache for me," Lilith said. "But, how many times have you nearly died trying to help me out?" Lilith asked. "I can't die. But, still you risk everything. You've only got one life."

"That backfired," John said. "I spent the night trying not to get killed by you."

"I tried," Lilith said. Her shoulders slumped. "I thought we established that I'm not a good person."

"But you could be." John stopped. "Why try and turn me into leather and then turn around and save me?"

"You're my friend." Lilith sighed. "I didn't want to eat you."

John's brow furrowed. "Funny way to show it. Go on."

"When your blood hit my skull in the septic tank it started the regeneration process. I have to eat what starts it all or I go crazy." She shoved her hands in her pockets and stared at the ground.

"Like, losing all your blood and chasing me through the streets of American Fork, crazy?" John started walking again. They reached the intersection of State Street and 900 West.

"Yes," Lilith said. "Sorry about that." She pushed the button for the crosswalk, and then pushed it again. "How did I lose the blood?"

"Lisa drained you." John stared across the road at the signal.

"Did I eat Lisa?" Lilith asked.

"Yep."

"Oh," she melted even further, the self-recrimination almost audible to the outside world. "I need to tell you something about Sarah. Lisa killed her."

The signal changed, and John crossed the road.

"That sucks," he shoved his hands in his pockets.

"Yeah," Lilith said.

They walked in silence past the plasma center to John's apartment complex. Together they stood at the bottom of the stairs to John's place.

"Fine." John tossed his hands in the air and marched up the stairs.

"What?" Lilith raised a brow, but she stayed at the bottom.

"I've already taken on a hodag," John continued, "Why not add an irrational immortal to the mix."

"I'm not a pet," Lilith glared at him.

"No, you're my friend," John said. "But friends don't use potions, spells, or magic on each other." He listed them off on his fingers and walked down the stairs. "Right?"

"Yeah, you're right," she said.

"I'm going to need help with the hodag and whatever else comes my way," he said. His backpack shuddered and twitched.

"That's it?" She walked up the stairs. "That's easy."

John rolled his eyes as she passed.

"I get the shower first," Lilith stood by the door, waiting for him to open it.

"Why do you get the shower first?" John asked, opening the front door. "It's my bathroom."

Lilith gestured at herself. Blood matted hair, torn clothes, and an assortment of garbage that decorated her like glitter. "I smell the worst," she said. "And if you don't let me go first, I'm going to rub myself all over your furniture while I wait."

John groaned. "Fine!"

Lilith slapped his shoulder as she entered. "And then let's get some food. I'm starving."

ACKNOWLEDGMENTS

I always read the acknowledgements in a book. You get to see behind the scenes of how a story came to be. Acknowledgements just like a good story have reoccurring elements. Authors tend to have an amazing support team, and an overwhelming sense of gratitude for those that helped get the book finished and their own unique journey. I'm not any different, everyone who has helped make this book happen has my gratitude and I hope they know how important they are to me. Whether they were directly or indirectly involved with the process.

First off to my parents. They instilled a love of reading in me from a very young age. As a kid I loved hearing the stories about the adventures that have made up their lives and I'm proud to be a part of that. My siblings for having my back throughout the process whether it was hanging out with their niece and nephew, so I could get some work done. Or for sharing their knowledge on a topic I may not have been so knowledgeable on.

Some of my favorite memories from when I was younger were from trips to the Public Library. Libraries have always been a haven for me and I love that they allowed me access to some of the best books. To Sister. Hooper and Sister. Coffey my high school librarians who always had a kind smile or recommendation for a book to read. I didn't feel like a stranger when I was in the library.

I've always had a love for English Literature a big part of that is thanks to Sis. Crawford my high school English teacher who I felt believed in me and that I was capable of amazing things. I have had some amazing teachers and professors in my life and I'm grateful for their time and efforts to help me to continue to grow and progress.

To the team at Dragon Steel (Especially Kara and Mem) thank you for letting me volunteer with signings and shipping. Being able to be behind the scenes has taught me a lot about publishing and how to be awesome. Also having the opportunity to sit in on Brandon Sanderson's BYU writing class helped not only this book but my own skills as a writer. Thank you for being willing to share your knowledge and experience. If it weren't for this class I wouldn't have The Wereslugs (Amryn Scott, Dallan Simper, Jessica Allen Winn and Mark Chiba) who helped save this book from some abysmal world building, structure and grammar issues. An extra shot out to Amryn for being an extra set of eyes for the manuscript.

Here's to the Merchant Prince of Fandom Alexi Vandenberg who has been more helpful than he realizes. Bard's Tower is a unique experience. As a writer I've loved being able to talk and bounce ideas with some of the most amazing authors in publishing today. Bringing readers and authors togethers is one of the great joys of my job and I'm grateful to be able to make that happen.

My editor Micki Cottam took on the challenge of a first novel. You will have a new goat soon. I promise.

I love my family and I appreciate their support. Jon has probably read, this manuscript more times than he'd care to admit. But he encouraged me to keep going. I'm grateful for the laughter and smiles of Kasia and Jack.

You've made it to the end of my acknowledgements. But there is one last acknowledgement. Dear reader, thank you for reading my novel, it means a lot to me.

ABOUT THE AUTHOR

Erika Kuta Marler currently resides in the state of Utah with her family.

You can find Kuta Marler online at:
www.kutamarler.com

 facebook.com/KutaMarler

twitter.com/EAKM

instagram.com/kuta1of7

Made in the USA
Columbia, SC
19 June 2018